MURDER ON THE ROCKS . . .

Suddenly the frigid town of Tromsø was one of the hottest spots in Norway. It all began when Professor Mackenzie's dog started sniffing around in the snow and uncovered a human ear —attached to a stark naked corpse. After three months on ice the trail was as cold as the climate. But Inspector Fagermo refused to give up. He soon discovered that the death of a stranger was just the tip of the iceberg—and that beneath Tromsø's frozen surface lay a dangerous conspiracy of blackmail, espionage, and cold-blooded murder.

"DEFT CHARACTERIZATION . . . A PLEASURABLE POLICE PROCEDURAL WITH A CHILLY ZEST."

—*The Plain Dealer* (Cleveland)

Scene Of The Crime ® Mysteries

2 A MEDIUM FOR MURDER, Mignon Warner
4 DEATH OF A MYSTERY WRITER,
Robert Barnard
6 DEATH AFTER BREAKFAST, Hugh Pentecost
8 THE POISONED CHOCOLATES CASE,
Anthony Berkeley
10 A SPRIG OF SEA LAVENDER, J.R.L. Anderson
12 WATSON'S CHOICE, Gladys Mitchell
14 SPENCE AND THE HOLIDAY MURDERS,
Michael Allen
16 THE TAROT MURDERS, Mignon Warner
18 DEATH ON THE HIGH C'S, Robert Barnard
20 WINKING AT THE BRIM, Gladys Mitchell
22 TRIAL AND ERROR, Anthony Berkeley
24 RANDOM KILLER, Hugh Pentecost
26 SPENCE AT THE BLUE BAZAAR, Michael Allen
28 GENTLY WITH THE INNOCENTS, Alan Hunter
30 THE JUDAS PAIR, Jonathan Gash
32 DEATH OF A LITERARY WIDOW, Robert Barnard
34 THE TWELVE DEATHS OF CHRISTMAS,
Marian Babson
36 GOLD BY GEMINI, Jonathan Gash
38 LANDED GENTLY, Alan Hunter
40 MURDER, MURDER LITTLE STAR,
Marian Babson
42 DEATH IN A COLD CLIMATE, Robert Barnard

Murder Ink ® Mysteries

1 DEATH IN THE MORNING, Sheila Radley
3 THE BRANDENBURG HOTEL,
Pauline Glen Winslow
5 McGARR AND THE SIENESE CONSPIRACY,
Bartholomew Gill
7 THE RED HOUSE MYSTERY, A. A. Milne
9 THE MINUTEMAN MURDERS, Jane Langton
11 MY FOE OUTSTRETCH'D BENEATH THE TREE,
V. C. Clinton-Baddeley
13 GUILT EDGED, W. J. Burley
15 COPPER GOLD, Pauline Glen Winslow
17 MANY DEADLY RETURNS, Patricia Moyes
19 McGARR AT THE DUBLIN HORSE SHOW,
Bartholomew Gill
21 DEATH AND LETTERS, Elizabeth Daly
23 ONLY A MATTER OF TIME,
V. C. Clinton-Baddeley
25 WYCLIFFE AND THE PEA-GREEN BOAT,
W. J. Burley
27 ANY SHAPE OR FORM, Elizabeth Daly
29 COFFIN SCARCELY USED, Colin Watson
31 THE CHIEF INSPECTOR'S DAUGHTER,
Sheila Radley
33 PREMEDICATED MURDER, Douglas Clark
35 NO CASE FOR THE POLICE,
V. C. Clinton-Baddeley
37 JUST WHAT THE DOCTOR ORDERED,
Colin Watson
39 DANGEROUS DAVIES, Leslie Thomas
41 GIMMEL FLASK, Douglas Clark

A Scene Of The Crime® Mystery

DEATH IN
A COLD CLIMATE

Robert Barnard

A DELL BOOK

Published by
Dell Publishing Co., Inc.
1 Dag Hammarskjold Plaza
New York, New York 10017

ISBN: 0-440-11829-8

Reprinted by arrangement with Charles Scribner's Sons.
Printed in the United States of America

First Dell printing—April 1982

CONTENTS

CHAPTER I Twilight at Noon 9

CHAPTER II Domestic and Foreign 14

CHAPTER III First Light 26

CHAPTER IV Deep Frozen 42

CHAPTER V Mortuary Matters 45

CHAPTER VI Reluctant Witnesses 59

CHAPTER VII Husband and Wife 72

CHAPTER VIII Two Girls 84

CHAPTER IX No Place 98

CHAPTER X Work and Play 108

CHAPTER XI Marital Relations 120

CHAPTER XII One Day 134

CHAPTER XIII The Cardinal's Hat 146

CHAPTER XIV Wife of a Friend 159

CHAPTER XV Blood in the *Vindfang* 176

CHAPTER XVI Illumination 187

CHAPTER XVII Midnight Sun 217

AUTHOR'S NOTE

Setting a book in a real town always involves the danger that the reader will assume that the characters as well as the topography are based on reality. I should like to insist, therefore, with even more force than usual, that though I have remained fairly faithful to the geographical facts in depicting Tromsø, the characters are entirely fictitious: the policemen are not Tromsø policemen, the students are not Tromsø students, and above all the Professor of English is not Tromsø's Professor of English.

CHAPTER 1

TWILIGHT AT NOON

Seen from the windows of the café, the main street assumed an aspect less than solid, though more than shadow. The light, such as it was, had a temporary, unwilling feeling to it. The sky had earlier been faintly tinged with a pallid blue, but haze and cloud had robbed it by now of any suggestion of daylight. The wooden cathedral looked large, a solid, comfortable mass, but its features and those of the main street of wooden shops were as if under mufflers, to be seen only indistinctly. The people, hurrying over the gritty snow and ice, were interested solely in getting where they were going. The day, such as it was, would last no more than an hour or so, and then everything would be wrapped up in fitting, natural darkness.

It was midday on December 21 in the city of Tromsø, three degrees north of the Arctic Circle.

The boy standing by a table and stripping off his anorak and scarf seemed to be deciding that he'd had enough of the city for the moment. He looked at the faint glow of light outlining the shops and offices, like a faded halo around a grimy saint, and then looked down at his newspaper. Something caught his eye on page one, and he took it with him to the counter. Absently he took a tray from the pile, collected on a plate a ham smørbrød and a cheese roll, and then made himself a sort of cup of tea, with a bag and some near-boiling water.

'To-og-tyve nitti,' said the woman at the cash desk, pressing the keys. The boy looked at her for a moment, before fumbling in the back pocket of his jeans. 'Twenty-two, ninety,' the woman said in careful English. The boy counted out the money slowly, then carried the tray over to his table.

Half an hour later he had digested his paper and his meal and drunk his tea, but he did not seem inclined to go. He fetched another cup of tea and sat over it, looking yet not looking out at the twilit town. There were things going round in his head, but too many things: sometimes he frowned, as if trying to work something out, or trying to dismiss from his mind something he did not want to think about. As his tea got cooler and cooler, he sat there, staring, unseeing.

He was about twenty-two. His hair was fair, but with a rich, golden fairness that was not Norwegian. His face was lean, old for his years, and his eyes—when they were registering anything—looked slightly calculating. His hands were rough as sandpaper, with stubby fingers, and his nails cut close and dirty. He sat in his jeans and his bulky, shapeless sweater, gazing at the ashtray, in which his teabag was mingling to a disgusting mush with the ash and butts.

In fact, he was hardly even thinking. Impressions, memories of the last few days, swam sharply to the front of his mind, then retreated to become part of the great wash of recollection. The woman, blonde, desperate, and the nerve in her cheek that twitched as she asked him round for coffee . . . The American girl, horribly earnest, confiding her emotional problems, as she confided them, he guessed, to friend and total stranger, indiscriminately . . . The cellar pub, with the alcove where everyone spoke English and tried to make in that corner of a foreign field that fuzz of togetherness which is an English country pub . . . The dreadful Professor of whatever it was, with the Dracula teeth and the watchful eyes.

His mind turned to the business in hand, and his eyes contracted from infinity to the here and now. He looked at his watch. Twenty past one. The appointment was for half past two. He had no desire to walk and re-walk the main street of Tromsø until it was time to get a bus or a taxi. But perhaps he could walk to the place. He looked out of the window; it had not started to snow, though it threatened. It would pass the time. And on the way he could think the matter through. He had a feeling he had been too casual—had started something that could get out of hand.

He took out his map and spread it over the table. It was across the bridge, he knew that. A fair distance then, but easy enough to manage if the roads were all right.

'Can I help you? Anywhere you want to go?' asked a voice.

The boy looked up. A middle-aged man with a tray—kindly-faced, probably not trying to pick him up. Still . . . He replied coldly: 'No, I'm just looking.'

The man went on to another table, discomfited.

The boy drew his finger over the bridge. Here things were less built-up, it seemed. His finger fol-

lowed the main roads on the other side of the bridge
until suddenly it lighted on his destination: Isbjørnvei.
If he were outside, he thought, he could probably see
the house across the water. He judged the distance
with expert appraisal. He could walk slowly and still
do it easily. He stood up, tallish, slight, but tough-
looking, and began swathing himself in his anorak and
long woollen scarf—multi-coloured in stripes, the
product, perhaps, of some unstoppable girlfriend or
mother.

Out in the street, in a world of bright shop windows
and street lights surrounded by looming shadows, he
set his face towards Storgate, and walked along it for
the last time, he hoped, that day. He idled, noting the
decorations for Christmas in the shops and the Christmas trees oddly decorated with the Norwegian flag,
as if Christ had been born in a stable near Oslo. He
bought a hot dog, and stood for some time munching
it and staring ahead of him at the shoppers, streaming
this way and that. When he had finished eating, he
patted his anorak, heard the crinkle of paper from his
inside pocket, and went on his way again, reassured.

Now he was nearing the bridge. Underfoot the
snow and ice were grimy and gritty, but he wore
heavy boots, the soles deeply rutted, and there was no
danger of sliding or falling. The footpath over the
bridge was very narrow, and the traffic passed unpleasantly close, but he paused when he reached its
highest point, the wind biting through his too light
trousers, and looked back to the island on which
Tromsø is built, and then out to the other islands,
mere sleeping monsters in the distance, guarding the
deep. The fjord sent back dull twinklings from the

dying day and the lights of the city. Impassively he turned on his way.

Once he reached the mainland he lingered around the Arctic Cathedral, two great white triangles, and peered in the windows. The place held no memories for him, and he dawdled on. Up the road, with the traffic grazing his ankles, then to his right and a long, quiet, straight walk to his destination.

It was a quarter past two when he neared the end of Anton Jakobsensvei and began to turn down to Isbjørnvei. There were a couple of people walking and the occasional car, but by now the light was all but gone. The moon had come up, round the mountain behind him. 'Darkness at Noon'—the phrase went round in his head. He stopped and considered. The walk had not sorted out his thoughts and he was aware he needed to decide what to do—not knowing how little use there was in his meditation.

Then, finally, in the gathering dark, he walked down and found Isbjørnvei. The name was dimly lit on the side of a house, and he walked along the road, peering at the numbers. The snow was rather roughly cleared here, and many of the paths to the houses not swept at all. He trudged rather than walked. Finally he came to No. 18, made his way through heavy snow up the path to the door, and rang the bell. He turned on the doorstep while he waited, and looked once more over the fjord to the white and coloured lights of the town.

Nobody had seen him come. Nobody saw him again alive, except for the person whose footsteps in the house he now heard, and whom, turning, he saw as the door opened.

CHAPTER 2

DOMESTIC AND FOREIGN

Sidsel Korvald was—all her friends agreed—a model Norwegian wife. Her house was always spotless: the windows, upstairs and down, were cleaned (with some publicity) once a month, and the curtains washed nearly as often; the dishes were never allowed to stand over from one meal to the next, and if the children played in the living-room, their mother made clear to them the difference between a pleasant sort of disorder and a mess. Her husband's meals were invariably ready for the table the moment he came home from work, and were never more than mildly experimental, ringing the changes from sausage, to meat-balls, to cod, and pork chops, invariably served with boiled potatoes. Her mother had impressed on Sidsel that one thing the menfolk could not stand was novelty in their diet. The children were kept quiet while her husband slept off his meal, and coffee was waiting for him when he woke. At weekends she made herself genteelly desirable for bedtime, and was sweetly co-operative on any other day of the week.

Her husband hated her very much indeed.

Affection had declined into boredom almost before the honeymoon was over; pity succeeded boredom, irritation pity, and hatred had come after eight or nine years of marriage. Then Bjørn Korvald knew the time had come to move out.

On that day, December 22, he had been alone in his tiny flat off Kirkegårdsveien for three months, and the magic of separation had still not worn off. Everything he did seemed to be invested with a new significance. When he came home from work the pleasure of cooking for himself renewed itself every day, and unpacking the things he had bought for the meal gave him a piercing, unnatural delight. Deciding how to cook it was an intellectual treat and an adventure—especially as he avoided sausage, meat-balls, cod and pork chops, from instincts very close to superstition. When he had eaten, he piled up the dishes on the tiny draining-board, and finished off his beer. Sometimes he listened to a record, and as he did so he walked around the flat and looked at everything, sometimes even touching the cheap or second-hand furniture as if it were the concrete evidence of his liberation. Sometimes he laughed out loud for no reason.

Today he did things with the same relish as ever, but he did not laugh. He had decided to take his Christmas presents to his children, and he did not expect the visit to go easily. His wife had greeted his decision to leave her with a stunned bewilderment, like a puppy left for the first time in kennels during the family holiday. Before he left it seemed as if a smouldering anger was succeeding the bewilderment. Since then his contacts with her had been limited to formal greetings when he went to collect the children every Saturday for his ration of their time. All the financial arrangements were done through the bank, with computerized impersonality. He did not know how Sidsel was standing up to the separation, and in his heart of hearts he did not want to know. Sometimes, in the middle of the night, he was terrified at the way he had hardened his heart. But he did not think that she, any more than he, wanted any extended contact, and in fact when he stood on the doorstep, gaudy boxes in hand, and she opened the door to him, her words were:

'Oh. Do you want to come in?'

'Just for a moment,' he said diffidently.

He shook the light dusting of snow off his overcoat, and took off his shoes by the front door. He caught his wife looking at his stockinged feet, and remembered that she always did like guests to bring slippers with them. He weathered the excited rush of his little girls and bore them upstairs to the living-room, his wife following behind.

The house was as it always had been: every little piece of brass was shining, every surface immaculately dusted, the carpet clean, glossy, its pile unnaturally erect. Everything was as usual, but Bjørn Korvald, perhaps oversensitive, thought he detected now in his wife's cleanliness a note of desperation, of fanaticism. Was it boredom, was it a visible piece of bravado, was she defiantly asserting that she was not abandoning her standards, was it done especially in anticipation of his visit, to remind him that she had always made him a very good wife?

He wished he could care. Sidsel had seated herself neatly in the other armchair, and when the little girls had borne off their parcels to their bedroom, to be

16

gazed at and gloated over as part of their pile of bright paper packages, Bjørn took up the last parcel and (feeling the deadly fungus of hypocrisy clutching round his heart) said: 'For you.'

'Oh. Thank you very much,' she said, glancing at it, and putting it neatly on the side table. It was, Bjørn thought, about as much as it deserved.

'Are you managing all right?' he asked.

'Oh yes, perfectly well, thank you,' she said, with an impersonal polite smile, as if he were a welfare visitor.

'Is there anything I can do for you before Christmas?' he asked, battering against her blandness without quite knowing why. 'Anything you want fetched, any wood chopped?'

'No, I don't think so,' she said, as before.

'Of course, I could come round on Christmas Eve ...' he said, his heart in his mouth in case she accepted.

'No,' she said calmly. 'It would only disturb the children. They're just getting used to the situation. It will be better for you to have them on Boxing Day, as we arranged.'

He said to himself: she hopes I will be lonely. 'Well, if you're sure you can cope—' he said.

'Oh yes, I can manage quite well.' Her blonde, china impassivity never faltered, and her mouth was firmly set in an expression of sweet resignation. Her husband edged himself forward in his chair.

'Have you thought of taking a part-time job?' he asked. He had not intended to ask it—it was one of those things that flash into the mind and are out before they can be considered.

17

'Certainly not,' said his wife, her tone immediately edgy with opposition. 'I suppose you're thinking of the money. You forget that Karen isn't five yet. I've never had any time for these women who go out and leave their children all day with just anyone. My business is here, making a home for them.' She looked him coldly in the eye. 'Especially now,' she added.

'Of course, if you feel like that about it . . . It wasn't the money—I thought you might find time hanging heavy. Thought you might be better for an outside interest.'

She looked at him with the old, painful bewilderment on her face, genuinely not understanding. 'But I have the home,' she said. Suddenly he saw in her left cheek that involuntary nerve twitching, as it had in the few crises of their marriage. It gave her a cruelly lop-sided look. 'I have friends,' she said; the pitch of her voice suggested carefully controlled hysteria. 'I'm not lonely. I'm as free as you are, remember.'

But Bjørn Korvald knew she was desperately lonely. Had she had a man round, invited him round, scared him off, perhaps, by that strange new desperation? The thought did nothing to him, but he thought it was time to go, before antipathy reverted to pity. Luckily his wife made the move.

'I think you'd better go now,' she said, seeming unhappy that the beautiful china mask had slipped a fraction.

'Yes. It is getting on. Perhaps if I can tiptoe out I needn't disturb the children.' He saw his wife looking down at his stockinged feet, as if he could do nothing else. She was always wonderfully good at making one apologetic. He slipped on his overcoat and shoes, and his wife opened the door for him. Standing there in the doorway, having regained all her blonde impersonality, she had as much individuality for him as an air hostess on a short-hop flight, and he had as much difficulty as any passenger in framing words of goodbye.

'Well—Happy Christmas,' he said.

Sidsel Korvald smiled, a yuletide frosting over the face, and closed the door. As he walked down the path, meticulously cleared of snow, a great wave of relief that the visit was over swept through him. He decided to celebrate by catching the bus into town and going to the Foreigners' Club.

Tromsø, properly considered, is the Norwegian equivalent of an outback town. To the east stretch the great open spaces of Finnmark, and the Russian border—the country of Lapps, mosquitoes, and the hardier breed of tourist. To the north, west and south are fjord and islands and fishing grounds. It is the gateway to the Arctic, but that is not a portal many have cared to go through. Its history is of fishing and whaling and subsistence agriculture, and it is only in the last decades that it has expanded, with pockets of industry, a university, and the threat of oil. Its expansion has made it a city of exiles, vaguely nostalgic for the sun of East Norway, or the rain of Bergen. It has also acquired a rich sprinkling of foreigners.

The Foreigners' Club as such met once a month, for talks and musical evenings and little plays. The lonelier foreigners came there to meet, drink beer and coffee, and talk over with the others the iniquities of the Norwegian immigration laws and all the things one couldn't buy in Tromsø. But the club proper had an illegitimate offspring which met informally most evenings in the Cardinal's Hat, a Dickensian, cellar-like restaurant, where members ate snacks, drank beer and talked English, in a corner which by tradition had come to be reserved for them. Here the foreigners were often joined by Norwegians who liked to practise their English, or who had nostalgic memories from the war. Bjørn Korvald, who worked with a shipping company that ran one of the daily coastal steamers up the west coast of Norway, had plenty to do with tourists in the summer, and liked to stop himself from getting rusty in winter. An occasional visit to the Cardinal's Hat had become an agreeable variation on the pleasures of newly-won solitude.

Tonight the crop of English speakers was not very promising. Coming with his beer and hamburger over to the dark, wood-walled corner, with cushioned benches round the wall and two or three tables, he found only four people, and these included two young Americans deep in the sort of conversation only young Americans can ever get into.

'I have this problem relating to people,' said the girl—shabbily dressed as if by conviction, with a thin, peaky, worried face and hair all anyhow—desperately earnest and (Bjørn suspected) hideously boring. She paused to throw a 'Hi!' in his direction, as if marking him down for future use, and then went back to her subject, speaking low and devoutly, as if at confession. 'I do think the socialization aspect is vital, don't you, Steve?'

'Right,' said Steve, without conviction. He was a

boy in his early twenties, beanpole-thin, and gazing
dejectedly down the expanse of dirty tee-shirt covering his upper half.

'I just flunk out, somehow. I just never make the
grade. I mean—well, how do I affect you? What sort
of person do I strike you as, frankly, Steve?'

'Sort of average.'

'Yeah, well, you see. It's always like that. I don't re-
ciprocate easily. I have such a restricted social set-up.
I try to get in contact with people, and I just bomb . . .'

The possibilities for breast-beating on the topic
seemed endless and infinitely dreary, and Bjørn, sink-
ing down on to the bench by the girl, turned to his
other neighbours.

Helge Ottesen was a local businessman, with a
men's outfitters just off the main street. He was small,
plump, balding, genial, hand-rubbing, and moderately
trustworthy. His wife Gladys, acquired from Essex
during the war, was matronly, jolly, and had a sort of
English High-Street smartness about her, which
showed she had kept contact with home. Bjørn knew
the pair well. Helge had gone into local politics a few
years ago, and now—in his fifties—was a leading light
of the Tromsø Conservative Party, and constantly active to keep that light shining bright. Gladys revelled
in the activity, and strove with all her jovial energy to
play the part of Mary Ann to his Disraeli.

'Nice to see you, Bjørn,' said Helge, speaking in
English, as was the custom of the place. 'How are you
keeping? What have you been doing with yourself?'
His bald head glistened reflections from the wall
lamp, and his teeth flashed tradesman's sincerity.

'Well, actually, I've just been taking Christmas presents round to the family,' said Bjørn Korvald. Helge Ottesen's face collapsed in several directions. He was a man who liked situations where one could be jolly, optimistic and encouraging, and he shunned death, disease and financial collapse as things unsuited to his personal philosophy of life. Separation was one of those nastily ambiguous things that upset him most: did one commiserate, or did one dig roguishly in the ribs? Anyway, Sidsel Korvald's father was a good customer of his. He tried to put his face into neutral.

'It's awful for the kiddies,' said his wife comfortably. 'But there, it might be worse if you stayed together, that's what I always say. How's the tourist trade?'

Helge Ottesen brightened up immediately. His wife was a jewel like that, and always knew how to steer the conversation round from the emotional uncertainties that he hated to subjects where his own particular brand of bonhomie could operate.

'Yes—how about it?' he said. 'I hear it's likely to be a good year, eh?'

'I expect so,' said Bjørn. 'Bookings are very good. Of course they always are. But the season seems to be lengthening. The boats are filling up from Easter on, and the bookings go on into late September. It makes up for the off-season.'

'Yes, pity about the off-season,' said Helge, consoling himself with a sip of whiskey. 'Nothing much came of the attempt to attract a Christmas trade, did it?'

'You mean "Spend Christmas in the Land of the

Midnight Sun"? No. It wasn't really honest, and most people saw through it too easily.'

'Pity, that. I'd have thought Americans might have gone for it.'

'Once perhaps. That sort of trade's no good.'

Helge Ottesen looked uncertain again. 'Anyway, as businessmen, we've got to admit that things aren't all that bad. Lots more trade than there was ten years ago, and if the oil comes, things will get better and better.'

'In one way, perhaps,' said Bjørn dubiously.

Helge Ottesen did not like doubt to be cast on the great god oil, and became almost polemical. 'You mark my words,' he said. 'In spite of what people say, it'll transform the whole of North Norway!'

'That is precisely what people do say,' said Bjørn. 'That's what they're afraid of.'

'That's just the carpers, the professional trouble-makers. They said the same about the university, but it's done wonders for this town. The people there have money to spend.' He looked at the scraggy American boy with the dirty sweat-shirt and the jeans genuinely rather than artificially aged. 'Not that they always do spend it,' he added sadly.

The exploration of personality problems at the next table was still in full swing, and involuntarily they paused to listen.

'Some people like they just walk into a room and pow! everyone smiles, they feel better, they really do. When I go in, they just kinda wilt. Know what I mean, Steve?'

'Errgh.'

23

'Somehow I'm just not self-actualized. I mean, what do people say about me? What kind of social reciprocation do you think I set up?'

'You piss people off,' said Steve. He looked up momentarily from his gloomy contemplation of his beer, as if he half hoped the girl would burst into tears and dash out into the night. But in fact there was an expression on her face of the deepest masochistic satisfaction.

'Exactly,' she said. 'Now I need to analyse those reactions, you see, and . . .'

Helge Ottesen had listened to this conversation as if he could not believe his ears. He shook his head, and looked uncertainly from Bjørn to his wife and back again. 'I don't think I understand young people any more,' he whispered plaintively.

'They're not all like that,' said his wife comfortably, sucking the lemon from her drink. 'You meet lots of nice young people around.'

'That's true,' said her husband, brightening. 'You meet lots at the Club, and we've had some of them home, haven't we, Gladys? That's where the Club is so useful.' Helge Ottesen was a vice-president of the Foreigners' Club, and was used to defending it to his fellow townsmen who didn't particularly like the influx from abroad or want them to feel at home in Tromsø. 'We bring them together, and make sure they're welcome. Then there's this place, too.'

'That's right,' said his wife. 'There was that English boy came in here the other night—two or three nights ago. Quite by accident, and heard us talking English. He seemed a nice type.'

'That's right,' said her husband, subsiding into contentment. 'He was a pleasant chap, fitted in very nicely. I think he enjoyed himself. He didn't say what he was doing here, but at least Tromsø gave him a great welcome.'

He smiled happily into his glass at the thought of Tromsø's great welcome.

CHAPTER 3

FIRST LIGHT

On January 20 the sky over Tromsø was clear at midday, and the sun showed gloriously but briefly on the horizon and splashed orange gold over the fjord. All over town little ladies had coffee with each other in celebration, and men in shops and offices who had missed it because they forgot to look up from their desks nevertheless said that they had seen it, and how nice it was to have it back. Life, everybody felt, was returning.

For the men on duty at the Tromsø police station it was a day like any other. The only ones who glimpsed the returning sun were those out in twos patrolling the streets—and that was very few, for the police in Norway prefer that crime should come to them, rather than that they should go out looking for it. Most of the men in the large square building down from the Cathedral laboured over paperwork in quadruplicate, lounged over coffee with their mates, or typed with their two index fingers lengthy and impressionistically-spelt reports. In the office near the main door where the general public was received Sergeant Ekland, square and dark, and Sergeant Hyland, square and dark, stood fingering their square, dark, droopy moustaches, modelled on a television policeman, and thinking what a fine pair of fellows they were.

It was shortly after twelve-fifteen, as the sun disappeared in a final liquid flicker and Tromsø re-entered its familiar twilight state, that the office door opened and a little old man entered with an odd walk, half cocky and half defensive—the walk of a man who is trying to say he has nothing to fear from the police, and is saying it none too convincingly. He was not particularly clean and not at all well shaven—the whitish stubble bristling defiantly round his sunken mouth and his nicotine-stained teeth. He was half carrying and half dragging a large knapsack attached to a metal frame—a type of burden much used by Norwegian hikers and campers, who like to carry their life history round with them.

'I can't stop, I'm busy,' he said, dragging his burden over to the centre of the office.

'Nobody asked you to stop, grandad,' said Sergeant Ekland, magnificently bored.

'I've got *middag* to prepare,' went on the old man, as if he hadn't heard.

'Crowded out with guests, are you, Mr Botilsrud?' asked Sergeant Hyland, sardonically as he thought. Old Botilsrud was proprietor of the *pensjonat* up near the swimming pool, a rather dirty, musty affair that did well enough in summer when all the other hotels and boarding-houses were packed out. Botilsrud was suspected (and more) of selling bottles of spirits to his guests at laughably high prices without the licence that made that sort of robbery legal, and though the suspicion had never actually led to charges being

27

brought against him, the two sergeants felt they could dispense with their usual thin veneer of respect.

'I've got guests,' said the old man defiantly. 'Casual workers,' he went on, his face falling. 'Scum. Anyway, what I've come about's this knapsack.'

'So we see,' said Sergeant Ekland. 'What's it all about? What's in it? Empty bottles?'

'There's not much in it,' said Botilsrud, once more cultivating deafness to insinuation. 'I looked, just to check, but there was nothing worth—nothing much in it. It was left by this lad who stayed up there at my place. Just left it behind, he did.'

'When was this, grandad?'

'Matter of a month or so ago. Just before Christmas, it was. I'm not sure of the exact dates, because my books got in a bit of a muddle about then.'

'I'll bet,' said Sergeant Hyland. 'Festive season and all.'

'Anyway,' said Botilsrud, preparing to leave, 'I thought I should bring it in, because he disappeared.'

'Here, hold on, grandad—your guests will have to wait for their princely meal. You can't just dump this here and go off. We have to get something down on paper. Now—what exactly do you mean, disappeared?'

'Well,' said Botilsrud impatiently, 'as far as I recollect, he said he was staying three nights. Then after the second I saw nothing more of him, not sight nor sound. He took the room key, too, and I never had it back.'

'Had he paid?'

'Oh yes,' said the old man, with a look of feeble cunning. 'I made sure he paid in advance. I always

28

do—have to, with some of the types you get coming to this town.'

'OK, then, what was he like?' said Sergeant Ekland, taking a pencil and paper, and only pausing to smooth lovingly his splendid black moustache with the back of his hand, as a prelude to composition.

'Well, sort of ordinary, really. About your height or a bit taller, but not so bulky. Very slender, really, I'd describe him as. Then his hair: well, it was fair—yellow fair, you know what I mean? Not white fair. What was he wearing, now? Oh yes—jeans and a check shirt, same as they all do—they've no imagination, young people today. That's about all, really. Oh yes, and of course he was foreign.'

'Foreign?' Sergeant Ekland perked up. Foreigners were always of some interest in Tromsø, due to its closeness to the Russian border, and the politically sensitive area of Svalbard. And Christmas was not a time one would expect many foreign visitors in North Norway. 'What kind of foreign?' he asked.

'How would I know? English, perhaps, or German.'

'You should have details of his passport.'

'I told you, my records got jumbled,' said the old man. Sergeant Ekland sighed a great big theatrical sigh. To placate him, Botilsrud said: 'Anyway, he wasn't American.'

'That's very helpful,' chipped in Sergeant Hyland. 'How do you know that?'

'Anyone can tell an American,' said the old man contemptuously. 'You can hear.'

'But he spoke Norwegian?'

'He had a bit. Enough to hire a room. Otherwise,'

said the old man grandly, 'I'd have known what nationality he was.'

'Hmm,' said Sergeant Hyland. Coming round to the front of the counter, he humped the knapsack up, and vaguely began to turn over its contents. They were not very interesting. 'Just clothes,' he said. 'Change of shirt, vest and underpants, a pair of boots. Not much.' He peered closly at the shirt. 'No identification marks or name tags. You're not giving us much to go on, grandad. I suppose you nicked all the diamond rings and the stolen Rembrandts, eh?'

'He-he,' said Botilsrud unenthusiastically. 'Look, I've got to get back.'

'O.K., O.K., get back to your beef stroganoff,' said Sergeant Ekland. 'I expect the boy just did a bunk, or got a girl or something. But we can put a bit in the paper, and see if anything turns up.'

And as old Botilsrud edged out, crabwise, to the street, Sergeant Hyland heaved the knapsack into the corner and went back to contemplating his image in the plate glass door, while Sergeant Ekland tucked his tongue between his lips and began composing for the newspapers a three-line paragraph about a missing person.

It had made a break in the monotony of the morning.

Sidsel Korvald had got up heavily, given the children breakfast, got the elder off to school, put several layers of clothing on the younger and sent it out to play in the snow, and then began brewing her second cup of coffee of the morning. She trudged through the dusting of new snow to the letter-box and fetched the morning paper, then she poured the thick black liquid into a large breakfast cup, took three lumps of sugar from the packet in the cupboard, and settled down on the sofa to read the paper.

Or rather, she did not settle down, and did not read. She had not settled down—ever, she felt—since her husband moved out; since the humiliating, inexplicable day when he left her. She had gone about the house doing the usual things, behaving as if nothing had happened. But she knew that everything had happened, nothing was the same. Her body felt stiff, as if poised to receive another blow. It was so unfair, so *wrong*. It was the sort of thing that happened to women who had been bad wives. It had happened to people she knew, and she had often sympathized with the husband. But she had been a good wife, none better. She looked around her house now, and suddenly it wore a completely new air. Suddenly it was a desert of labour-saving appliances—and for what? She did not want to be saved labour. She had all the time in the world. Her very shopping had suffered: she had bought in bulk before the price went *down*; she had fallen for several crazy non-bargains. She told herself that things would get back to normal before long. But she could not imagine what was 'normal' for a single woman with children. She felt reality slipping through her fingers, day by day.

She tried to concentrate on *Nordlys*. Sport she skipped over, the foreign page she did not so much as glance at. She tried to read the leader on North Sea oil, but lost the thread; then she tried to take in all the little items of local interest which were the staple of the newspaper, and which had always roused what in-

terest she could take in things outside herself, her
family and her home. The grievances of fishermen,
the lack of doctors in North Norway, the doings of the
radical students—she read them, and did not read
them, her mind elsewhere, anywhere. She registered a
heading, 'Missing person', and was about to move on
to something else, when her eye caught the description:

> Foreign, possibly German or British. Was in the
> Tromsø area 19th-21st December. Height—about
> 1m 80. Slender build, fair hair . . .

She paused. The dates had caught her attention, and
the nationalities. She uncrossed her legs suddenly, and
jolted the coffee table. Coffee spilt from the cup on
to the polished wood surface, but she did not, as normally she would, rush for a cloth to mop it up. She got
up, tenser than ever, and went towards the window.
Outside her youngest was fighting with the boy next
door, but she did nothing, merely looked unseeing.
But over her face there had spread a vivid crimson
blush.

Helge Ottesen was late into the shop that morning.
He had to go to a Town Council meeting in the evening, and was expecting a hard day. He prided himself on being able to delegate authority, though he
took all the important decisions himself. The shop
would run itself, while he enjoyed a late breakfast. He
and his wife divided the paper in two, and retreated
into companionable silence, he at the same time

spreading a piece of bread with marmalade, and stirring the thick coffee which was the first of his daily necessities.

'Helge,' said Gladys Ottesen from the other side of the table. 'Listen to this.' And in her slightly cockney Norwegian she read out the heading 'Missing person', and the description of the boy.

'Could be anybody,' said her husband, hardly looking up from the sports page.

'But don't you remember that boy who came into the Cardinal's Hat, just before Christmas? He joined us in the foreigners' corner, and we had a bit of a yarn—you can't have forgotten.'

'Why should it be him?'

'Well, the description: English—then the height, I'm good at heights—' (Gladys worked now and then in her husband's menswear shop)—'and the fair hair. The date's about right too, because I remember that when we met him I'd just been Christmas shopping, getting in the last-minute things. So it all fits, really. Do you think we should go along to the police?'

Her husband looked at her with those wonderfully frank businessman's eyes of his.

'Why should we get mixed up in it, Gladys? It doesn't do any good, politically or any other way. And after all, we only met him for a couple of hours, if that. What information could we give the police that would be any use?'

His wife sipped her coffee and nodded her head. 'Yes, I suppose you're right. Even if it *was* him, there's nothing much we could tell them, is there?'

Helge Ottesen returned to his newspaper with a

grunt of assent. He'd said it before, and he said it now: his wife was an invaluable woman, absolutely invaluable.

Steve Cooling was eating dinner out for a change. The Pepper Pot was the best restaurant in town, and eating there was something of an extravagance, but Steve had had a largish cheque from home that day, and the cheque had coincided with his finishing the penultimate chapter of his thesis. It seemed worth a minor celebration, so he sat eating reindeer, drinking a half-bottle of red wine, and vaguely peering now and then at the local paper.

Steve was from the State of Iowa, and was working for a year in the History Department at Tromsø, completing a Ph.D. on emigration from North Norway to the States. He liked the University of Tromsø. It was small, like the one he had come from, and one could put up with a lot, weather-wise, to be in a place where everyone knew everyone else. Looking around the Pepper Pot he found he knew nearly half the people there: there were students who had just received their loans and were blowing a hundred kroner as a good start to the term; there were people from the University Administration, ordering North Norwegian specialities for a sceptical-looking distinguished guest; and there were members of the academic staff, some single, some presumably escaping for a night from Norwegian Home Cooking (a curse called down upon good food to rob it of all taste and texture), and all of them scanning the menu earnestly, as though it were *Middlemarch*. Among the academics, in fact, was the Professor of English Literature, sitting at the table next to Steve, talking and eating an enormous meal, and not properly separating the two activities. He was watched with a degree of ascetic disgust by a young-ish lecturer in French.

Professor Halvard Nicolaisen was thin, gaunt, unattractive: his face was like a face in a spoon, sunken, cratered, an area of dark corners and uninviting crannies. His manner, when he was most natural, was gloomy and intense, which he tried to cover with dreadful jokes, jokes which lasted minutes because he embellished them with Victorian convolutions of plot and syntax. His laugh was high and unamused. When he ate, he showed two brown Dracula fangs on either side of his mouth, for he did not close it properly and breathed fragments of food over his companion. He was now—as he usually was—deep in the minutiae of university politics.

'This matter of starting Finnish,' he was saying, in a lowered voice thick with food and conspiracy. 'I wanted to get your opinion, since you're on University Council.'

'I haven't really—'

'It's a mistake. It'll never catch on. It's the sort of thing the radical students cry up, but none of them will think of taking it.' He waved a meaty fork at his companion and leaned forward, fixing his despondent eyes on him. 'It's not in your interest, either. Too many small languages competing for not enough students.'

'Of course that is one thing I—'

'Right. Now, if we can come to some agreement, work together, make some plan of campaign . . .'

35

The two of them sank without trace into the mire of university intrigue, and Steve savoured the last scraps of his meal. With one half of his mind he read his paper, while with the other half he planned the broad outlines of his last chapter, with its magisterial summing-up of economic factors and regional trends. It was when he was thinking his way into his final paragraph—misty and grand—that his eye caught the tiny item about the missing person. He read it through, then read it again. It pulled him up with such a start that, without thinking or considering whether it was the right thing to do, he drained his glass, pushed back his chair, and made his way over to the next table.

'Excuse me—' he said.

The two academics surfaced, blinking. The French lecturer looked as grateful as Wimsey being hauled out of a bog. Professor Nicolaisen, on the other hand, fixed Steve with a cold eye, pursed his thin lips with irritation, and simply said: 'Well?'

Professor Nicolaisen spoke in English, but it was his only concession. Steve could see he had made a mistake. At the Cardinal's Hat Professor Nicolaisen affected good fellowship, attempted a meagre heartiness. It was, clearly, a role which was for there alone, and not part of the serious business of his life.

'I don't want to butt in, Professor,' said Steve, hesitating, 'but I just saw this in the paper.' He was committed now. Professor Nicolaisen, twitching his long thin nose with irritation, accepted the paper, took with great show his glasses from his pocket, polished them, and put them magisterially on. Then he read wearily through the item. When he had finished, showing no vestige of emotion, he folded the paper and handed it back.

'Well?' he said again. The word was not an invitation to explain, but a rebuke. Steve plunged further in.

'You remember that boy who came into the Cardinal's Hat just before Christmas. An English boy—he said he was just in Tromsø for a couple of days.'

'I can't say I do.' The voice was high and precise.

'You were there, I remember. And your wife came in.' Professor Nicolaisen blinked his eyes in extreme irritation, as if Steve had somehow committed a *faux pas*. 'He was a fair-haired boy, in his early twenties, and about that height.'

'Fair-haired young men are not uncommon in this country,' said Professor Nicolaisen with a weary sigh.

'He was foreign,' said Steve, his face flushing slightly. 'How many foreign fair-haired boys of that height do you think were in Tromsø on exactly that date?'

'I wouldn't like to guess. Perhaps you could try the Mathematics Department.' Professor Nicolaisen looked at his guest and attempted one of his countertenor laughs. Then he turned his glacial eyes back on Steve. 'Really, I can't see why you should interrupt me with this. I understand young people are very—' intake of breath, indicative of distaste—'mobile these days. It is part, is it not, of their—' another quick intake—'*life-style*. No doubt the young man just—moved on.'

Steve repressed a desire to say: 'In the middle of December?' Instead he just murmured: 'Possibly. If so, he left his luggage behind.'

'Oh, no doubt there was some—*girl* or other,' said Professor Nicolaisen.

'So you don't think I should go to the police?'

'You must do as you think best, of course. I shouldn't think it would be anything to get involved in, not as a *guest* in this country. But you must use your own judgement about that, naturally. As I was saying—'

Professor Nicolaisen turned back to his companion, with a gesture of dismissal.

Steve Cooling went back to his table, dissatisfied, and settled his bill. He had hardly been helped by the conversation. But he got the same sort of answer half an hour later, when he went along to the Cardinal's Hat for his coffee. He was hoping (for once) to meet Nan Bryson, the American girl with the problem of relating, and there she was alone, stewing over a long-drawn-out litre of beer, and scanning the horizon for acquaintances as if they were ships passing her desert island.

'Steve!' she cried in a pitiable wail, as if she had just killed the thing she loved. 'You've been avoiding me, and I know why. I deserve it, I know it. I can't *tell* you how sorry I am I bored the *pants* off you last time you were here. Going on and on about *myself*. Just *stop* me, Steve, when I do that, because I *tell* myself not to, and then I go and do it every *time*. So just *stop* me—'

'Oh, that's all right,' mumbled Steve.

'I'm not going to say one word tonight, Steve, not a word. Now—what about you? How do you tick over? Tell me about yourself, just for a change.'

Steve Cooling tried to begin to tell her that he would find that conversation almost as boring as he had found the last, but he gave up. Nan Bryson was too irredeemably personal to understand what he meant. Instead he pushed the paper in her direction, tapping the paragraph with his finger.

'Hey,' she said when she had read it. 'Isn't that the guy that was in here?'

'Right,' said Steve, relieved at her promptness.

'Just before Christmas, I remember it well. Dates are right, and everything.'

'You and he had something going, didn't you?'

'We *did*.' Her face lit up for a moment, then slipped back to its usual doubtful misery. 'Or I *thought* we did. Actually, to tell it to you straight, we made a date. Right here, we made a date. He was coming round to my flat.'

'And—?'

'Well—' Nan Bryson turned down the corners of her mouth in an expression of despair, half real, half play-acting. 'He broke it, tell you the truth. It cut me up, because I liked him, I really did.'

'He seems to have disappeared about the twenty-first,' said Steve, looking down at the paragraph in *Nordlys*. 'Was that about when you had the date?'

The girl's grubby, thin little face puckered in thought, then she swooped down into a great big untidy shoulder bag by her feet, fished in it for some minutes (dumping some rather embarrassing personal items on the table in the process) and finally surfaced with a pocket diary.

'Still got last year's,' she explained. 'This year hasn't

39

done much for me yet.' She flicked through the pages. 'Hey, yeah. It was the twenty-first he was supposed to come. That evening. Reckon that's why he didn't show up?'

'Could be. Maybe we should go to the police.'

The girl's face fell again.

'Oh hell, Steve, I wouldn't want to do that.'

'Why not? They're asking for information.'

'Well—I'm kinda ashamed.' She pulled herself up. The young will never admit to shame. 'Not ashamed, sort of embarrassed. I made a bit of a set at him—like you saw. I guess you knew what was going on. Then he didn't show up, and I felt kinda cheap.'

'What if he didn't show up because he disappeared?'

'Well, even so, I don't feel that much better about it. I wouldn't want to talk about it. Then there's my job, you see.' She looked meaningfully at Steve. Light dawned. Nan Bryson had a part-time job with the United States Information Office in the town, generally considered a far-flung outpost of the CIA. 'We're supposed to keep a very low profile. There's enough talk about us at the moment—you know how it is.'

'But hell—if you just went along with information—'

'That's getting involved. And if I'm put out on my ear, what then? No job, no work, no work permit. It's back to the States for me. No, Steve, I'd like to help, honestly I would, but just keep my name out of it, can't you?'

And so in the end Steve Cooling, like the rest, did nothing. The paragraph in *Nordlys* caused a little trickle of comment and speculation, especially in the foreign community, but it seeped gradually down into the fjord, and was buffeted by the currents till it finally sank. Quite soon it was replaced by other topics of interest. The year wore on, the weather grew milder, and the sun gained confidence enough to stay in the sky for several hours a day.

CHAPTER 4

DEEP FROZEN

In the late afternoon sun, a man and his dog walked up past the Arctic Cathedral towards Anton Jakobsensvei. It was the second week of March. There had been an unexpected early thaw the week before, and the black of the road stood out against the prevailing white—as, too, did the bright daffodil-yellow patches on the snowy verges, part of the great dog postal network. There was hardly a soul about. The Norwegians had mostly had their Sunday constitutional, and had retreated home for their Sunday *middag*. As the man walked along, the extractor fans of various houses flung out to the cold afternoon air odours of meatballs in tomato sauce, fried cod and roast pork in gluttonous profusion.

The man was medium height, slight but running to tummy, with fat red cheeks and a splendid furry hat. He had skis on his shoulder, carried somewhat inexpertly. The dog was brown and nondescript—a sort of basic dog, but perky and interested. They proceeded spasmodically, from daffodil patch to daffodil patch. The sun shone on them, watery but welcome.

They turned into Anton Jakobsensvei—past the supermarket, past the Ebenezer chapel with the long icicles hanging from its guttering, cold as nonconformist charity, past the road up to the cable car. A few stragglers were stepping it out manfully from the bottom station back home to eat. These were not going up the mountain to ski, however: that was for experts. They went on, past the houses for naval officers, and then, just before the turn-off down to Isbjørnvei (where the man had lived for a time, when he came here from the Middle East), up towards the mountain. Here there were open spaces and gentle slopes. Now was the time of little light; now was the time when the younger members of the family finally dragged themselves in for television children's hour; now was the time when the novice skier could get in a little practice on the easier slopes, unembarrassed by kindly adults or frankly contemptuous children.

The brown dog, already excited at the recognition of old haunts, became delirious as they turned off the road into the snow and he was let off his lead. The snow here was not too thick, after a mild winter and the recent thaw. Along the best paths it had been nicely packed down by skiers. The man walked a bit, away from the lights of the road, and turned towards the increasing gloom. The dog went around inconsequently, on and off the ski tracks, sniffing, giving little yelps of recognition, and sometimes bounding off at nothing. Eventually the man unloaded his skis from his shoulder, and began inexpertly the business of getting them on his feet.

It's just a bloody clumsy way of walking, he said to himself.

While he fumbled with the straps his eye caught a moving black shape to his right. There was a man some hundreds of yards away, skiing down the mountain. Damn. He'd expected to be alone. He fussed over the straps once more, determined to take his time. The skier would soon be past him and on to the road, and then he could begin an exploratory practice.

A sharp bark. Another—questioning, uncertain, summoning. Come and tell me what to do about this, you. The man looked up, one ski on, one still half off. The dog was now just a dark shape against the snow. He was barking, whining, approaching, looking round, digging furiously, looking round again, wagging his tail experimentally. The man, his skis now on, stood up and cautiously moved forward. As he did so, the skier from the mountain also neared the dog and swerved to make a classy halt. The dog now was more confident, and had begun tugging at something.

The two men came together, and the owner called 'Jingle', without much confidence, clearly not expecting to be obeyed. The dog looked at him, then went on tugging, backing away, then going back to tug again. In the gathering gloom the two men went forward, to get a closer look at what he had got hold of.

It was a human ear.

CHAPTER 5

MORTUARY MATTERS

No body looks its best in a morgue. There is something abstract, wholesale, impersonal about the setting which robs the corpse of individuality or pathos. It requires an effort of the imagination to summon up the sympathetic responses that would have come unbidden if the body had been seen resting its last rest on a bed or in a coffin.

The body that had been found on the snowy slopes behind Anton Jakobsensvei lay in the long, cold room in the university's Medical Department, which served as the morgue of the Tromsø Police Force. It was naked, as it had been found. No scrap of clothing or possible identifying object had been left on it. Some damage had been done to the right ear, but it was nothing to the damage done to the back of the skull, which had been smashed in by a single blow from a heavy implement. It was the body of a young man, just under six feet in height, fair-haired, slim. In other circumstances one might have felt he was 'carrying back bright to the coiner the mintage of man'. Now he was just a body on a slab in a police morgue.

Standing by the body and looking at it with the police surgeon was Inspector Fagermo of the Tromsø police. He had one of those fair, unlined, age-less Norwegian heads. How old was he? Perhaps somewhere between thirty-five and forty-five. But if he had said twenty-eight or fifty-five one would hardly have been surprised. It was a good face, decep-tively sleepy but regular, intelligent, blue-eyed; only the occasional crinkling at the edges of the mouth sig-nified the presence of a sense of humour that was un-Norwegian in its irony and blackness.

The mouth crinkled now. 'Would you care to hazard an opinion as to the cause of death?' he asked.

The police surgeon, who liked his humour cosy, folksy and conventional, merely pursed his lips and fixed his eyes on the smash at the back of the skull. Jokes were of his life a thing apart—they were Fager-mo's whole existence.

'There's something about that body,' Fagermo went on. 'The shape. Look at those thighs and calves. Thin, aren't they? The chest too, though he looks a healthy young chap. He doesn't look like a skier, does he?'

'Is there any reason why he should be one?'

'People don't usually go skiing naked, agreed—not at this time of year anyway. Still, most of the young people around here do ski . . .'

'Are there any young people missing from around here?'

'There are always missing young people. You find they've gone to sea, or to the university, or something . . . That fair hair, now—it's almost yellow, isn't it? Very unusual. Have you had a look at his teeth?'

'I've had the body no more than a few minutes,' said the surgeon, rather snappily. He went to the head and peered into the jaws. The body was still half

46

frozen, and he was careful not to disturb the gaping wound at the back of the skull. He took a torch and shone it into the slightly open mouth.

'You could be right,' he said at last. 'There's dental work there that doesn't look Norwegian. I'll be able to tell you more when I've had a more thorough look.'

Fagermo went on looking, his lips pursed as he considered the boy's way of death. 'Whoever did it,' he said at last, 'clearly didn't want it identified. He stripped off everything before he took it out and buried it in the snow. Including a ring, you notice. It could have been a fairly messy business.'

'He could have been naked when it was done,' objected the police surgeon.

'It's a possibility, but I fancy not,' said Fagermo. 'Look at the neck. There seems a definite line to the blood from the wound—as if it's been stopped by something: a shirt, a jacket, something fairly tight that's later been removed.'

'If so, it could certainly have been messy,' said the surgeon.

'So the longer the body is unidentified, the better our friend will like it,' mused Fagermo. 'I think this calls for a bit of inspired guesswork . . . Wasn't there a missing persons ad from us in the paper five or six weeks ago? Some tourist or other, I seem to remember—a young lad.'

'Search me,' said the police surgeon. 'I wait for trouble to come to me.'

Fagermo looked at him with his characteristic look of somnolent humour, and went outside to his car. He put it in gear, and did the two-minute drive back to the station. There he went through to the inner office, a large but windowless room, rather smoky and smelly. Here was where most of the policemen in Tromsø spent much of their time during their spells of weekday duty (it was the weekends that were rich in hooliganism and drunkenness, and then they could sometimes be seen on the streets). And here they mostly were now, shirt-sleeved and feet up.

'Who's missing?' said Fagermo casually as he went in, looking around from under his heavy lids.

'That's what we were just discussing,' said one young constable, with some traces of eagerness still in him. 'There was that young Fagertun boy—'

'He ran away because his father knocked him around,' said Fagermo. 'Don't blame him either—we should have locked the man up years ago if we'd had any gumption. We'll find he's got a job on a boat I wouldn't mind betting. In any case he's much too young—only fifteen or sixteen, and I seem to remember the description said dark. What about foreigners?'

'Foreigners?' There was a general vacant look.

'You know, Germans, Englishmen, Americans, people who come from overseas,' said Fagermo in a deceptively helpful manner.

There was a general pause for heavy cogitation.

'There was that boy,' finally said Sergeant Hyland, stroking his superb dark moustache and looking wise. 'That boy we put out a notice about.'

'Yes?'

'Old Botilsrud at the Alfheim Pensjonat came in about him. Don't think there was anything in it myself. Boy had obviously cut off with some girl. He'd left behind a knapsack, but that didn't mean much, because there was very little in it. We put out the notice just in case, but nobody's come along.'

'But he was foreign?'

'So Botilsrud said. Couldn't put a nationality to it, though. Of course his records were all to pot.'

'Get Botilsrud,' said Fagermo. And as Sergeant Hyland casually finished off his cup of coffee and started looking for his cap he added in a whiplash voice: 'Fast!'

As Sergeant Hyland went through the door in as near as he liked to get to a hurry, Fagermo said: 'I'll be next door. I'd better have a chat to the chappies who found him, though I don't suppose they can know anything of much interest.'

In the waiting-room next door the rather weedy man with the fat red cheeks and incipient tummy was sitting with his brown dog at his feet—the dog crouched forward, his head between his paws, suspicious and melancholy, painfully convinced that kennels were in the offing, or an injection, or some other dimly remembered canine disaster. By them sat the other witness to the discovery of the body—a well-set-up man of thirty-five or so, sporty, and half in, half out of ski gear. They were talking a weird mixture of Norwegian and English, in which they were misunderstanding each other very amiably.

'Ah,' said Fagermo to the Englishman, and sticking to English for safety's sake, 'now it was you who found the body, wasn't it?'

'Well—him really,' said the man, pointing to his dog, who brushed the dusty floor with a tentative wag of the tail. 'He was making such a fuss I had to go over

49

and look. Then Captain—what was it?—Horten came down, and we both more or less found it together.'

'I see. And you are—?'

'My name's Mackenzie. Dougal Mackenzie. I'm a Reader in Marine Geology at the university.'

'And I'm with the navy, of course,' said Captain Horten.

'Good,' said Fagermo. Well, when you'd seen it was a body, what did you do next?'

'Well, we didn't disturb anything—that's very important, isn't it?'

'Oh yes. Though it would be more important if we thought he was lured naked under some pretence or other and killed there on the spot, but that seems unlikely. Still, at that stage you could hardly know.'

'No—we didn't realize.' The Englishman's face had fallen. 'We only waited to see that the ear was joined to a head, if you see what I mean. Not just a stray ear. Anyway, we put Jingle on his lead—I hope he didn't damage the body—and then one of us had to ring for the police. Captain Horten lives in Anton Jakobsensvei, only a minute or so away, so he went and I stayed on guard. Then the police came and took over.'

'I see. Well, I don't suppose there's any more help you can give. Have you seen the body?'

'Yes,' said Horten. 'We both cut off home for a bite to eat, then came along here. They took us over to see—it—soon after they brought it in. I'm afraid I can't help: I've never seen him before.'

'And you?' said Fagermo, turning hopefully to the Englishman.

'No, never,' said Dougal Mackenzie. 'It's not one of my students.'

'You thought it looked like a student, did you?'

'Well, he looked about the right age, that's all. And I'd heard there'd been several student suicides recently, though you seem to hush them up in this country.'

'Hmm,' said Fagermo, not too pleased with the expression 'hush up'. 'Well, if that wound on the back of his head was caused by the lad himself, he'd have made his fortune in a circus. I won't keep you, but we'll certainly be needing you for the inquest. If you'll both just leave your addresses in the outer office . . .'

In the outer office, and making a superb fuss about it, was old Botilsrud from the Alfheim Pensjonat. He had not changed his manner since January (any more than he appeared to have changed his clothes), but behind the shrill cantankerousness and crankiness Fagermo detected a degree of human relish which he recognized as all too familiar: it was the feeling that he might be in on something important, something sensational even, and the anticipation that it would provide material to bore his guests with as he served them meals and illegal drinks in the months to come. Such emotions Fagermo had come to recognize as among the less pleasant side-dishes to murder.

"This'll be a lesson to me,' he was saying in his high, thickly accented voice. 'Never give information to the police. Keep my mouth shut in future. I brought it on myself, and I'll take care not to do it again.'

'I hadn't noticed you made a habit of trotting along to us with gen about the criminal activities of your guests in the past,' said Sergeant Hyland in his world-weary voice. 'Quite the reverse seems to be the usual pattern, I'd say.'

'Dragged away in the middle of serving dessert—what does it look like, eh? Driven away in a police car. Most of my guests will have paid up and left by now.'

'What a refined type of clientele you must have,' said Hyland. 'You must have gone up in the world since I was last there.'

'Nonsense, Botilsrud, they'll be sitting up waiting for details,' said Fagermo, genially breaking in on the double act. 'Your guests aren't fazed by the word "police", if I know them. And I could even slip a word to the reporters about how helpful you've been.'

'Then everyone will assume I've done it, whatever it is,' grumbled Botilsrud.

'Come into my office, will you?' said Fagermo. 'No, wait: better come over to the morgue first.'

Botilsrud did not seem to have caught the last bit, for he muttered all the way out the main entrance: 'If you was to tell the reporters you was deeply indebted to me for promptly coming forward as soon as I noticed the disappearance and the invaluable assistance I've rendered since . . .'

'It doesn't sound like anything anyone would believe,' said Fagermo. 'We usually like to assume the public wants to be helpful.'

'Here, where are you taking me?' said Botilsrud, as he was hustled back into the police car.

'The morgue,' said Fagermo, and kept quiet until they got there, though Botilsrud kept up his aggrieved whine. Fagermo opened the door to the morgue and signalled to the police surgeon to cover the body to the neck.

'Oh,' said Botilsrud, looking through the door; 'it's a

body, is it? I thought it might be.' The idea did not seem to upset him.

'Yes, that's what morgues are for,' said Fagermo. 'Nothing too unpleasant, though.'

'Oh, I've seen bodies enough in my time,' said Botilsrud. 'In the war, you know. I was in the Resistance.'

'And never left it since,' said Fagermo. 'Now—do you recognize him?'

Botilsrud came close to the dead face and squinted at it for some seconds. It looked almost as if he were trying to smell his breath. Then he straightened and said: 'Yes, that's him. As far as I can say for sure. My eyesight's not so good as it was.'

'That'll do to be going on with,' said Fagermo. 'We might be able to get some more definite identification later on, when we have put a name to him. Let's go back to my office.'

They drove back again, and trailed up the cold stairs of the police station to Fagermo's office, this time Botilsrud making the journey in silence.

'Now,' said Fagermo as he closed the door, 'let me hear all you know about this boy.'

'I told Ekland and Hyland everything I know,' said Botilsrud. 'Why do you all want to waste my time? You could just go and look up their reports.'

'We didn't know then what we know now,' said Fagermo, mentally adding the rider: and Ekland and Hyland haven't got the brains of a pair of pea-hens. 'I gather since there was no name on the missing persons notice that you don't know his name. How come?'

'It was near Christmas. My lists were in a muddle.'

'Ah yes. Either through drink, or you're doing an income-tax fiddle. Not that that's anything I'm interested in. So this boy didn't book in advance, then?'

'He rang, as far as I remember,' said Botilsrud sullenly. 'I think he rang up from town, then turned up at my place half and hour later.'

'Ah ha—then he probably tried the hotels in town, found them full, and then went to the telephone directory. Might be worth making enquiries to see. Was this in the morning?'

'It's a long time ago now,' grumbled Botilsrud. 'It was a busy period. If you'd asked me in January, now . . .'

'What were you doing when he turned up?'

'Beds,' said Botilsrud, after a pause for concentration. 'Came down from doing the beds, and showed him straight to his room. So it must have been morning.'

'There, you see. If he'd arrived by coastal steamer he wouldn't get here till three. So if he came from any distance, he probably arrived by plane. Now—did you have any sort of conversation with him?'

'No. Why should I? I was busy. Anyway, the lad was foreign.'

'You don't know what nationality?'

'No—I told the sergeant. He spoke Norwegian, but he didn't have enough to have a conversation in.'

'Now that's interesting: just how much Norwegian did he have? Just a couple of phrases, for example—*takk* and *god dag*—a few things like that?'

'More than that,' said Botilsrud. 'He asked on the phone if I had a room—very slow, like, but it was in

54

Norwegian. And he seemed to understand what I said to him—when I told him the cost of the room, and said he had to pay in advance.'

'So perhaps a foreign student of Norwegian, or someone who'd been living here for a bit? Or would you expect a student to have a bit more than he had?'

'How would I know? I don't mix with students. Don't hold with them. Filth.'

Fagermo sighed. He looked down to the little clipping of the missing persons advertisement, which he had had sent up from records and which was now lying on his desk. 'O.K., then, let's just make sure of the details. He came on the nineteenth, is that right? And he paid you for three nights, meaning he intended to leave on the twenty-second, just before Christmas. But in fact he only slept in his room two nights.'

'That's right. Well—only one and a half, really. I heard him come in on the second night. I give them keys to the outside door, save me getting up. He didn't come in till three or half past.'

'How do you know? Were you still up?'

'Well, as it happened, I was. Some of the boys were making a night of it.'

'And you were making a packet out of them I suppose? O.K., O.K., ignore that. I don't care a damn what goes on at Christmas at the Alfheim Pensjonat—you can stage the Second Coming for all I care. But this night—the night of the twentieth it must have been— you were sober enough to remember the time he came in, were you?'

''Course I was. Doesn't do to get drunk with that type. I heard the front door open—we were in the kitchen to be more private, like—I opened the door just a crack, just to see who it was, and there he was, creeping in.'

'I presume you'd gone all quiet in case it was the police, eh, so he was afraid of waking anybody. Did you invite him in?'

'Not on your life.'

'Well, that's all very clear, very helpful. Now, what about the next day?'

'He got up late, as you'd expect. He was still in bed when I went up to make it, and I hadn't been early up. He must have gone out about half past eleven.'

'And that was the last time you saw him?'

'That's right.'

'Nothing to make you suspect he'd gone for good?'

'Nothing. Didn't take anything with him. Left his knapsack behind and just went off.'

'Only he probably *didn't*,' said Fagermo. 'I think we can take it that he was killed that day—the twenty-first.'

'Poor young bugger. Just before Christmas too.'

'Yes, well, let's hope he wasn't a practising Christian, shall we? Now, as far as you were concerned, that was it, was it? You talked to him on the phone, and when he arrived, and other than that you never exchanged a word?'

'That's right.'

'And on those two occasions the talk was only about practicalities—the room, the price, and so on?'

'That's right.'

'So he didn't eat with you?'

'No, no: he just had the single room. By the night.'

'And when he left, he left behind just what you brought in in the knapsack—nothing more?'

'What are you suggesting? There was just what there was in it when I brought it in.'

'Did the boy smoke?'

'Oh yes, he smoked.'

'Ah—you remember that. How?'

'He left one behind in a packet.'

'So he *did* leave something else behind?'

'Well, you couldn't count that, could you? I mean, not just a measly fag. And of course, I smoked it, so I couldn't bring it in, could I? You're not going to charge me for stealing one butt now, are you?'

'Do you remember the brand?'

'It was untipped, I remember that. Because I prefer the filters myself these days. One of those foreign brands.'

'Pall Mall?'

'No—one of those tight-packed kind. Don't see so many of them here these days, but there were lots who used to smoke them after the war.'

'Senior Service? Player's?'

'That's it. Player's. It was a good smoke.'

'I'm glad you enjoyed it. So the balance of probability is, he was British. Or perhaps from one of the colonies or whatever they call themselves these days?'

'Search me. Your job to find out things like that.'

'Quite right. And I'm most grateful to you for being so co-operative and forthcoming, Herr Botilsrud.'

Botilsrud looked at Fagermo closely, and saw only the bland, fair blankness which served him so well as a shield of his thoughts.

'Oh well,' said Botilsrud, cracking a smile across his own grimy face: 'Don't mention it. Any time. Here—tell your boys to lay off me for a bit, then, will you?'

And he shambled out.

CHAPTER 6

RELUCTANT WITNESSES

The morning began for Bjørn Korvald with five minutes of luxurious drowsing in his small, hard bed in the boxlike bedroom of his tiny flat. Reluctantly he heaved himself on to the cold vinyl and pattered into the kitchen to put on the coffee-pot. Then he blundered into the living-room and switched on the radio. The Norwegian Broadcasting Company was providing its usual morning blend of weather forecasts, news headlines, accordion music and religious indoctrination. Bjørn sliced bread, and fetched cheese and sardines from the fridge. Then he threw on a few clothes and slid down to the front gate to fetch *Nordlys* from the letter-box. He spread it on the table and began to read: the state of the fishing industry; oil exploration north of the sixty-second parallel; letters from crazy teetotalists; letters from dogmatic radicals; foreign news two days old. He browsed contentedly through the usual mixture, ate his sandwiches and then poured himself a second cup of coffee.

There were few items in the paper that could strictly be called news, and these were mostly of the cyclical, almost ritual kind which punctuated the passing year in Tromsø: someone had thrown himself off

59

the bridge; there had been drunken disturbances on Saturday night—windows had been broken in the centre of town and charges had been brought; the local theatre company was threatening to wind itself up. But there was one item, huddled down on the lower corner of the third page, that was something out of the ordinary. It had clearly been written in a hurry as the paper went to press: a body had been found buried in the snow out in Hungeren . . . murder was suspected . . . a man in his early twenties . . . fair-haired, 1.80 metres high. There were several misprints in the report, but the gist was clear.

As Bjørn walked down the street to his office in Grønnegate, sliding expertly over the icy patches as if his shoes were skis, his mind was active. Of course it was none of his business. And the body could be anybody's—though it was fairly clear from the report that the police did not know the identity. He'd heard of Steve Cooling's conjectures when that boy had been reported missing some weeks ago. He knew Steve hadn't gone to the police then. So far as he knew nobody else had either. Would anyone go along now?

Of course the police would probably make the connection between the two—but would they be able to find out who had spoken to him while he was in Tromsø? Not unless one of those who met him in the Cardinal's Hat went along to them. And since they seemed so disinclined, it might be worth while doing it for them.

When he arrived at his office he settled the morning paper down on his desk, open at page three, and pondered for a few minutes. Then he took up the phone and rang the police station. Jøstein Fagermo was one of his friends from schooldays—someone he met now and again around town, when they said 'long time no see' and how they ought to get together some time, but never got around to it, not from lack of liking but from laziness. On an inspiration Bjørn asked the switchboard operator for him.

'Hello, Bjørn, what can I do for you?'

'You're busy I can hear.'

'One hell of a case just landed in my lap.'

'Is it the body they found out in Hungeren?'

'Yes, it is. Know anything about it?'

'Well, no, only indirectly, but that's what I've rung about. Tell me, is it the same boy you advertised for some weeks ago? Fair-haired foreigner in his twenties, who disappeared round about Christmas?'

'Yes, it is. Or almost definitely it is. What do you know about him?'

'Not much. I never met him. But I did hear one or two things after the advertisement came out.'

'What sort of things?'

'Well, there's this American student called Cooling. He read the ad, and of course he couldn't be definite but it reminded him of a boy who'd come into the Cardinal's Hat just before Christmas and spent the evening there. I don't know if you know, but there's a table there where the foreigners collect and talk English—and a lot of Norwegians join them. I do myself sometimes. That's how I came to talk to this American boy. He'd been asking around the people who had spoken to this boy the night he came in, the ones who'd been sitting at the foreigners' table—asking whether they thought it could be the same boy, and whether he ought to go to the police.'

'And?'

'They all said no.'

'God damn people!' exploded Fagermo. 'What makes them treat us like lepers? Do we have some kind of collective bad breath, Bjørn? They run to us soon enough when the least little thing happens, wanting help and protection, but as soon as we ask for a little co-operation—'

'Keep your hair on, Jøstein, this isn't a press-conference. These were mostly foreigners, remember. Things haven't been so pleasant for them since the Immigration Ban. Several have been thrown out of the country.'

'Only if they were working without a permit . . . Well, let it pass for the moment. Did this American student know the boy's name?'

'No, I'm pretty sure he didn't.'

'Damn. Yanks are usually so good about names. They seem to have some sort of mental card-index for them. Did you hear who else was in the Cardinal's Hat that night?'

'Well, I know he went over and asked a couple of university people at the Pepper Pot—that was where he was eating when he read the ad. I don't know who they were, but he said they had both been at the foreigners' table when the boy came in. Then he mentioned a rather pathetic American girl—I think she works at the US Information Office. Quite likely she got the boy's name. I think there were some others, but you could ask him. Oh yes—he mentioned Ottesen the outfitter—you know, the chap on the Council.'

'What would he be there for?'

'He has an English wife. Anyway, a lot of Norwegians do join the table. I do myself.'

'Why?'

'Practise my English. And it's one of the few places you can go where people don't get into long arguments about the Norwegian language.'

'Point taken. You must invite me along.'

'Any time. But you must have better ways of making contact with these people. Sounds to me as if they may need a spot of intimidation.'

'You know we don't go in for that sort of thing, Bjørn. You've been listening to those people in the Sociology Department.'

'Anyway, I thought I'd let you know. It may save you a bit of time.'

'It will. I'm tied up with the medics most of the morning, and the scientific boys, and then I'm going to get on to Interpol and Scotland Yard. But when I'm through I'll have to follow up those names . . . Though, actually, I'm quite glad I can't do it right away.'

'Why?'

'Last time it was just a missing person. This time it's murder, and people will notice it and talk about it. It will be interesting to see how many of the people who met him contact *me* first . . . Bjørn?'

'Yes?'

'Could you go along to the Cardinal's Hat tonight?'

In the event, the only one of all those whom the dead man had met at the Cardinal's Hat to come to the police station of his own accord was Steve Cooling.

Shambling into the outer office, his bean-stalk body clad in dirty jeans and tee-shirt, an anorak, and a long woollen scarf, he looked sheepish and uncertain. Hyland and Ekland, officiating in the outer office, when they heard what he had come about took him down for a quick visit to the morgue (where Steve only nodded his head and swallowed ominously), and then passed him through to Fagermo. Steve sat down on the edge of a wooden chair on the other side of Fagermo's desk, looking intensely uncomfortable.

'I guess I should've come earlier,' he drawled.

'I *know* you should,' said Fagermo, without overdoing the heavy hand. 'You knew the ad was about the boy you'd met, you went around saying someone ought to go to the police, and in the end you never came.'

'Hell,' said Steve. 'How d'you know that?'

'Why didn't you come?'

'You know how it is . . . Everyone said they didn't want to get mixed up in it . . . In the end, I got scared, and sort of wondered whether I did.'

'You're not working here illegally?'

'Hell no. I'm not working at all. I'm writing a thesis. Would it have made any difference if I *had* come?'

'Probably not,' admitted Fagermo. 'I suppose we'd just have asked a few people who were there that night about him, then let it go. There was no body at that stage. We'd just have assumed he'd taken off somewhere, or gone home.'

'Yeah, well, that's what everybody said.'

'Everybody?'

'Well—people I talked to. The foreigners, and the Norwegians who come to the Foreigners' Club.'

'Is that a close little group?'

'Not specially. 'Course some of them stick together thick as flies on a bull's tail. But mostly we just meet when we meet.'

'Can you tell me who was there—at the Cardinal's Hat, I mean—on the night the boy came in?'

'I can, I reckon. Because I've been thinking it over, and talking with the others like I said. Right, here's the list, and this is just for the time I was there: the one he was talking to most was Nan Bryson—'

'Who's she? What does she do?'

'Nan—hell—she's American, she does odd things. She's typist at the US Information Office part of the time, then she does the odd private typing jobs and a bit of translation. She's not too hot at the translation. Her Norwegian's all right, but they complain about her English spelling and punctuation. She's kind of pathetic. She just about makes out, and that's all.'

'O.K., who else?'

'There were a couple of university guys. I know one of them's called Nicolaisen, but I don't know about the other. I think they're in languages. Pretty cold pair—look through you, know what I mean? One of them may come in when he reads the papers today.'

'They may. No sign of it so far.'

'They're kind of respectable, that's what I mean. Then there's this chap has a business in town, always smiling and rubbing his hands. Ottesen his name is. Some kind of men's shop—men's clothes. Has a plump English wife—quite friendly.'

'Yes, I know him.'

'Oh yeah—he's on the Council or something, isn't he? I suppose you would.'

'Anyone else?'

'Well, I think the Mormons dropped in briefly.'

'The Mormons?'

'Yeah, well, they didn't stay or sit down, and of course it's not their scene really, not being able to drink, and all, not even coffee. They were looking for someone, and they just stopped at our table and talked for a bit, just to be friendly. They don't give us the religion spiel—I think they're just lonely.'

'Too much competition in the way-out religions field up here, perhaps,' commented Fagermo.

'Right. Screwballs all over the place. Well, I think that's all, while I was there.'

'So the boy was still there when you left. Do you know whether he stayed long?'

'I guess so. Someone said he was still there pretty late on.'

'Now—what did you talk about? Did he say who he was?'

'No, I didn't hear him give a name, or any personal stuff. He just heard us talking English and came and joined us, but he didn't seem to know anyone there.'

'Hmmm. So he didn't even say where he'd come from, or why he was there?'

Steve creased his forehead. 'I've been trying to remember that. I know Trondheim was mentioned. And Bodø came up, and he said, "We've put in there." Or it might have been "We put in there"—like they'd called in on the way up on the coastal steamer.'

'Could be. But I rather think he came by plane. Would you say the boy had probably been working in Trondheim?'

'Hell,' said Steve, 'I just can't remember. I don't think he actually said that.'

'You think he was actually *working* in Norway, rather than just here on a visit, though?'

'Yeah, I guess so. We went up to the serving counter together one time, and the way he ordered and had his money ready—yeah, I guess he knew what he was doing.'

'Well, I suppose the Trondheim Aliens Office is a line of enquiry . . . Well, if you didn't talk about him, what did you talk about while he was there?'

'That's what I can't remember. I mean, we were talking when he arrived—you know, English Christmases, American Christmases, Norwegian Christmases—and he was mostly listening for a bit. People asked him how long he was in town, whether he liked it, where he was staying, but he was pretty quiet. You know how it is, when the others all know each other and you don't know anyone. Anyway, after a bit we sort of got into groups and then I didn't notice him any more.'

'And what group was he in?'

'Well, he was talking to Nan Bryson mostly.'

'You didn't hear what about?'

'There is only one subject with her—herself.'

'I can't wait to meet her. So you don't think he would have done much talking?'

'Just sat there paralysed like the rest of us, I guess.'

'Well, I suppose I'd best talk to her next, if I can get a word in edgeways.'

'I'll give you a tip: she had a date with him a night or two later, only he didn't turn up.'

'I think I can guess why,' said Fagermo.

* * *

The speed with which Nan Bryson appeared at the police station after he had rung her at the US Information Office gave Fagermo delusions of grandeur: he felt like a Senate Investigating Committee putting salt on the tail of the CIA. Did she feel guilty about not having come voluntarily, or was she booted down at high speed by her superior, who wanted the Office to remain as co-operative and inconspicuous as possible?

Fagermo felt less good twenty minutes later when, with less than no prompting towards autobiography, Nan Bryson had only come to the point in her life when she experienced feelings of rejection at play group. Fagermo felt that the case would be stale long before she had got through the more vividly remembered trials of her adolescence.

'That's fascinating,' he said, with his warmest smile. 'But I wonder if you could give me a bit more about what *he* said to you?'

'I was just trying to give you the atmosphere,' said Nan Bryson plaintively, the great ghostly brown eyes looking up at him like a spurned spaniel's. 'I thought it would be helpful—like how we came to be talking together, and the sort of thing we had going. But I guess you think it's just me droning on as usual. Stop me if I do it again.'

'Well, now—while you were telling him . . . all this, what was he saying?'

'I guess he was just saying "Yes?" and "Really?" and that sort of thing. You know how the English can say "Really?"—all cold and snooty.'

'You're quite sure he was English.'

'Oh yeah. He had that sort of glaze, like they have.'

'What exactly do you mean?'

'Well, I don't mean he was really snooty, not like upper-crust snooty. He was friendly enough on the surface. But he was a pretty cold guy. He didn't give any.'

'I see. Then what happened when you . . . exhausted that topic?'

'Well, I guess I said "Now tell me about yourself". I usually do—like I feel guilty. But by then they've had enough.'

'Was that what happened that night?'

Nan Bryson tried to remember. Clearly she had not thought over the encounter as Steve Cooling had—having in all probability had fresh fields and pastures new to occupy her mind. Finally she said: 'I think it was. By that stage it was getting fairly late, and things sort of tailed off.'

'Had he told you his name, by the way?'

'I think so . . . Hold it . . . What was it? Brown, that's it.'

Fagermo had seized his pencil eagerly, and now made a note in his book. 'And his Christian name?'

'Er—let me see. Charles . . . That's right, Charles.'

Fagermo put down his pen, and Nan Bryson fixed her great eyes upon him like a puppy who has tried to lick its master and been spurned. 'Is anything wrong?'

'The boy said Brown because if you say Smith people are immediately suspicious, and Brown and Jones are the next most common after that. Once he'd committed himself to Brown, he inevitably became Charlie Brown, but he disguised it a bit. If you'd woken up to it, he'd have pretended it was a joke.'

'Hey, that's real neat,' said Nan Bryson. 'But I thought I was telling you something really useful.'

'You were in a way. You told me that the boy wanted to hide his real name.'

'He *could* really have been Charlie Brown,' said Nan Bryson, as if unwilling to give up the idea of perfect honesty between them.

'And I could be Queen of Sweden,' said Fagermo. 'The boy wanted to keep his identity quiet—which suggests he was here for something crooked, or at any rate secret. He didn't give any indication?'

'No, none. He wasn't stupid.'

'I just thought,' said Fagermo carefully, 'that it might have had something to do with this US Information place you work at.'

Nan looked horrified. 'No—I'm *sure* it didn't. I mean I *told* him I worked there, and he didn't register at all. Gosh, you won't be pursuing that line, will you? I mean, I could get into trouble, and it's the only regular job I have. I mean they like to keep such a low profile, like practically *invisible*, you know . . . ?'

'I'll only pursue it if it seems likely to lead anywhere. I just thought you had contacts with some pretty odd characters, up and down the country, one way and another . . .'

'Oh, that's just what people *say*,' said Nan pleadingly.

Everyone knows it's a spy-ring, Fagermo felt like saying; the least secret one in the world. But he held his peace. There was no point in getting at an underdog on a matter like that. He said: 'Was the boy still there when you left the Cardinal's Hat?'

'Yes, he was. I've looked in my diary. I went to the

ten o'clock movies with a girl-friend. I remember he said he'd have another small one—so he was still around.'

'And the others were still there—the academics, the Ottesens, the Mormons?'

'Not the Mormons. They only dropped by for five minutes—I hardly noticed them, because I was talking. And Steve had gone. But the others were still there, I guess.'

'And you made a date with him, didn't you?'

Nan Bryson's face fell. 'Who told you that? Hell—it must have been Steve. Will I bitch into him about that.'

'We want to know *everything*, Miss Bryson.' What did they think this was? A spooky children's party game?

'Yeah,' conceded Nan, unconvinced, 'but it didn't come to anything, so it's kinda embarrassing.'

'What sort of date was this that you had? Was he coming to your flat?'

'Room really. Yes, he was. He was coming for coffee, we said, the evening of the twenty-first, about eight. That's why I feel sorta cheap. And then, when he didn't turn up, that made it worse. It's humiliating.'

'I doubt whether he could turn up, you know,' said Fagermo. 'I should think he was under two feet of snow.'

'Yeah,' said Nan Bryson. 'That's the best excuse anyone's ever had for standing me up.'

CHAPTER 7

HUSBAND AND WIFE

The rest of that day was a whirl of activity for Fagermo. Activity for him was not in itself unusual—though for many of his fellows in the Tromsø force it was—but the kind of activity was right out of the ordinary. Murder and manslaughter were certainly not unknown in the town, but they usually took very different forms from this: teen-agers now and then went too far in their weekend jollifications and did each other in in a playful manner; murderous lunatics were given temporary passes to the outside world from the local mental hospital and had a glorious time carving their families up, after which they were taken back, and the psychiatrists rubbed their hands together and said, 'We seem to have been a little premature,' smiling sad, gentle smiles. But murders mysterious, murders involving unknown assailants—more, unknown victims—these were very much outside the general run. Even Fagermo was not entirely sure how to proceed.

One of the things he did was to get an artist's impression of the dead boy's face, and get it sent hot foot to the local newspapers. The next thing he did was to send a detailed description to Interpol. Then he got on the phone to the Trondheim police station and dictated to them a series of detailed questions about aliens—aliens with police records, and above all aliens who had gone missing. An hour later they rang him back with a negative report.

'There's nobody missing that would fit the bill. Nobody that we *know* is missing, that is. All we have on our files are a middle-aged Italian musician and a pregnant German waitress. Both of them presumably have just gone home. Or possibly gone off together.'

'I see.'

'The point is, if his work permit wasn't up for renewal between Christmas and now, we wouldn't necessarily know he was missing. And even if he is on our books, he could easily have wound things up here, settled up with his landlord for his flat or whatever, and simply moved elsewhere.'

'He's supposed to notify change of address.'

'Yes, but the bastards seldom do—you know that.'

'The point is, this boy didn't just move: he got killed. I'd have expected some landlord or girl-friend to have been on to you with questions.'

'Well, nobody's come in here. Perhaps he wasn't intending to come back here after Tromsø anyway. What do you want us to do now? I suppose we could go through our records, start picking out likely names and checking up on them.'

'Yes—that's what I'd like.'

'It'll take time, as you know. And of course they'll all scream "victimization"!'

'You could confine yourself to men from the English-speaking countries, and I think you can cut out the States and Canada. They are usually recognizable when they try to speak Norwegian, and two of the people who spoke to him are quite positive that he wasn't American. Check on anyone between, say, eighteen and late twenties. Those are the outside limits. I'd have said early twenties myself.'

'That narrows it a bit. But we've got hundreds of the buggers here, remember.'

'I know. But make it top priority, will you?'

'Sure, sure,' said the voice at the other end, in an intonation Norwegians take on when wishing to convey that they wouldn't be hurried by the last trump itself.

This casualness on the part of the Trondheim police, this refusal to be unduly put out by other people's problems, was all the more aggravating the more Fagermo thought about the case, since he did not see how he could make a real start on essentials or make any significant progress before he had got for his corpse a name, a history, a personality. Here the boy was, murdered in a town in which he had just arrived—murdered, no doubt, by someone he met here, either by arrangement or by accident. But surely the *reason* for the killing must lie behind, lie elsewhere, in the boy's past. This was no casual knock on the head from a drunken teenager. The concealment of the body surely proved that. The investigation therefore had to be two-pronged: establishing precisely what the boy did during his two days in Tromsø; establishing his past and his personality, with a view to finding connecting links with Tromsø. Until he could get some lead on the second strand of the investigation—and surely the vital information must lie in Trondheim, or Britain, or at any rate elsewhere—then he would merely be marking time.

He looked down at the list of names of the people the boy had met at the Cardinal's Hat. The Ottesens would have to be approached cautiously: the kid-glove, would-you-be-so-gracious-as-to-spare-us-a-minute-of-your-valuable-time approach, as befitted a local Conservative councillor and a possible future Mayor. The Professor could be approached a little more freely, a man of title without power. He took from his bookshelf the University Catalogue and looked under Nicolaisen. There were three, under the various possible spellings, but two of them were women. The other was Professor of English Literature, and his address was in Isbjørnvei. Not more than two or three hundred yards from where the body was found. Interesting. Fagermo looked at his watch. Five-fifteen. Not the ideal time for a visit in Norway, but it looked as if today the gentleman was going to have his after-dinner nap interrupted.

As he was driven over the bridge in the direction of Hungeren where Professor Nicolaisen lived (and where the boy had found his long home) Fagermo noted walking down towards the bridge the two local Mormons, instantly recognizable figures. Always in twos, like Norwegian policemen, they wore dark grey suits in all weathers, with white shirts and neckties, and generally were impeccably turned out, as if their religion were an off-shoot of Wall Street, or at the lowest Savile Row. Fagermo looked curiously at the current representatives: both were healthy, prepossessing specimens as they all tended to be (what did they do with the unhealthy ones? Expose them on the Salt Lake?). These were clearly walking advertisements for their non-alcoholic and decaffeinated life-style. One was

75

think, chunky and serious, rather like a mortuary attendant in his dark suit and overcoat; the other was slim and fair, more carefree-looking, and with a tiny note of the careless in his dress: his tie was less than impeccably straight. He was looking around him with genial interest, while the other was looking directly ahead, his eyes on salvation, or the main chance, or something.

They can keep, thought Fagermo to himself. The Mormons are always with us. They can only have seen the chap for five minutes or so. Anyway it sounds as though he was talking to (or suffering conversation from) Nan Bryson at the time they came in.

Isbjørnvei was a new area of Tromsø, part of the opening-out that had taken place over the last ten years or so, and changed Tromsø from a large frontier outpost to a medium-sized country town. Little blocks of terraced houses had been built by various local interests around a small ring road, which thus divided itself into thirds: one third for navy personnel, one third for the university and one third for employees of the local council. These three groups existed apart, occasionally holding out the hand of sceptical friendship—rather like the Western and Eastern power blocs, and the Third World.

When Fagermo rang the door-bell at number twelve there was a longish pause. However, he was conscious of the pattering of socked feet upstairs, and sensed a face at the kitchen window looking down at the police car parked by the side of the road. Eventually the front door was opened by a long, gaunt, unattractive man with brown teeth and a manner which uneasily combined arrogance and uncertainty. The uncertainty was in this case probably aggravated by the nature of the visit: the man's expression, Fagermo felt, would have been positively hostile, if only he dared.

'Well?' he asked.

'Professor Nicolaisen?'

'Yes—' opening the door an inch further.

'I wonder if I might talk to you?'

'What about?'

Fagermo smiled in the friendliest possible manner, and said in a stentorian, neighbour-reaching voice: 'About the murder of the boy whose body was found up the back here yesterday.'

It was an infallible way of dealing with that sort of witness. The door was pulled hurriedly open, and he was ushered into the hall by a very flushed and flustered academic.

'What an extraordinary thing to do,' said Professor Nicolaisen.

Fagermo looked at him blandly, as if his words might refer to the murder, or anything else under the sun but his own actions. Professor Nicolaisen, further fussed by this lack of reaction or apology, led the way up the stairs which ended in his sitting-room. All the main rooms of the house were on this floor, and there hung around the room a faint smell of cooking—unpleasant, as if the food had not been very good, or well-cooked, or the meal not very sociable.

'You'd better sit down,' said Nicolaisen. He stood for a moment towering over him like a crumbling crag, seeming uncertain whether or not to offer him coffee. Then, deciding against it, he collapsed into a chair, like a block of flats in an earthquake, looking at him all the while gloomily, and glowering with some obscure resentment.

'Well?' he said again. The word was obviously one of *his* words, an off-putting ploy to put students at a disadvantage, socially and intellectually. His face was cratered with the scars of many battles—of easy victories over cocksure students, of sterile trench-warfare with colleagues over matters of principle. There was in his manner a nervous intensity which contained the odd mixture of aggression and defensiveness which rodents have, and those who engage in university politics.

Fagermo remained genially sociable. 'I don't know if you've seen the paper today?' he said.

'I've read *Aftenposten*.'

'Less exalted than that. The local papers both had a report of the body which was found up the back here yesterday.'

'Yes?'

'Perhaps you've heard of it?'

Professor Nicolaisen made a grudging admission. 'I did hear some talk of it yesterday. People saw the police cars around, I believe. But I was busy with a guest lecture I've been invited to give in Gøteborg. And in any case I would not have gone up to gawp.'

'That's a pity, now. You might have recognized the corpse.'

'Really? Hmm. A student, I suppose. Strange how the universities attract all the unstable types.'

'No, not a student. Or not one from here, at any rate. No, this is the boy that's been missing for some time. I believe the American student Steve Cooling

78

came and spoke to you about him in the Pepper Pot some weeks ago.'

'Oh yes? . . . I think I do have some vague recollection. But it was nothing to do with me.'

'But you had in fact met him?'

There was a pause, and then the same grudging assent, as if anything but contradiction came awkwardly to the man: 'I think we may have sat at the same table.'

'Exactly.' Fagermo smiled ingratiatingly. 'But you didn't come forward in answer to our advertisement.'

Professor Nicolaisen bristled. 'My God, I've had my office burgled three times in the last six months. On the last occasion they scattered my lecture notes out through the open window and defecated on the floor—and your men couldn't even be bothered to cross the road and give it a look. Why do you expect me to come running to do your work for you in those circumstances?'

Fagermo was unpleasantly conscious that—nasty though his manner was—the man had made a palpable hit. He decided he'd better not try to browbeat him, and became still more ingratiating.

'Well, well, I do take your point. Yes, indeed. Well, perhaps I could tell *you* when you met the boy. In fact, you were both of you in the Cardinal's Hat on the evening of December the nineteenth, and as you say, you both sat at the same table. You were with another member of the university, I think—?'

'Botner. Lecturer in French literature.'

'Ah, good. Now, I think you in particular should be able to help me. I've talked only to Americans so far—and you are something of an expert on English speech, so I've heard.'

Fagermo went thus far with the soft soap rather dubiously, since he thought the man might be too intelligent to respond, but he was gratified to see a faint relaxation of the cheek muscles—a near-smile of gratified vanity.

'Oh. You heard that . . . ?'

'Now, you must have some memory of how this boy spoke. Would you say he was English?'

Professor Nicolaisen sat back in a pose of contemplation, as if sitting for a bust of Milton. 'Ye-e-es,' he said finally, with lawyer-like deliberation. 'Ye-es, almost definitely, I'd say. I couldn't detect any trace of the colonial there—it almost always shows through.' It was as if he were talking of a stain on the tablecloth.

'*English*, you would say—rather than Scottish or Welsh?'

'Ye-e-es, yes, I'd say so.'

'Anything more precise? A Northerner, for example?'

The intellectual pose was intensified: *Paradise Lost* was in gestation. 'A Southerner, I'd say. And perhaps there was a trace of West Country there.'

Fagermo took this with a pinch of salt, as so much flim-flam, but he was glad his witness was mellowing into a better humour. He rubbed his hands with delight. 'Ah, now we're getting somewhere. Now—what sort of impression did the boy make on you?'

The response was very ready this time, and the good humour vanished. Professor Nicolaisen never spoke other than dismissively of the young: 'No particular impression at all,' he said. 'He was just a young man—someone who happened to drop in and join us. No great *force* of personality—' he smiled satirically—'that I can remember.'

'What did you talk about?'

'Good heavens, Inspector, this is months ago. I couldn't possibly remember. And I fancy I spoke to him very little. I was in conversation with Ottesen, I remember—sound man, not unintelligent. If I remember rightly, this boy was talking to some American girl: the young stick to the young, you know.'

It was unfortunate that at this moment the door from the hallway opened and a young woman walked in, clearly straight from the bedroom. She could hardly have been more than twenty-three, was blonde, sleepy and well-fleshed, with a jumper pulled over bra-less breasts, and tight jeans. Fagermo might have fallen into the unlucky assumption that this was Nicolaisen's daughter, had he not caught a glimpse of the man watching her with a greedy, untrustful look.

'A visitor, darling?' said the young woman in a bored voice, but looking at Fagermo appraisingly.

'Inspector—Fagermo?—yes—my wife Lise.'

She sat on the sofa opposite them, picked an apple from a bowl on the coffee table beside her, and bit into it, all the time watching Fagermo intently from under a Lauren Bacall lock of fair hair. He felt he was being added up like a column of figures. If she desired to make an effect, she certainly succeeded with Fagermo, for when Nicolaisen said rather testily: 'Where were we?' he couldn't for the life of him think, and for a moment there was an awkward pause.

'I suppose you were talking about the boy,' drawled Lise.

Fagermo turned to her quickly, and she added: 'The one they found up there,' jerking her head back towards the big window behind her as if she were talking of a lost cat or an elk strayed from the herd.

'You know about him?'

'Ye-es.' Her word was drawled with no sort of emotion, but no hesitation either. 'He's the one we met in the Cardinal's Hat.'

'I didn't know that you'd met him too. We've been enquiring about him for some time. I wish you'd come forward.'

'Didn't think about it,' she said, bored. In the silence her husband filled in nervously.

'My wife came to fetch me at the Cardinal's Hat. She'd been to a meeting, hadn't you, dear?'

'That's right,' said Lise Nicolaisen, and her gaze fixed itself on Fagermo with great intensity. 'Amnesty International.'

The gaze was unblinking, yet if anyone could be said to wink without moving an eyelid Fagermo would have said she had done it. How wonderful, he thought, to marry a young wife and be made a fool of by somebody half your age. Nicolaisen was plainly confused and uneasy.

'She just came in, and we—went, didn't we, dear?' The girl chewed steadily on her apple.

'And you left him there, did you, still talking to—who?—the Ottesens by then, I suppose?'

'That's right. The girl had gone a bit earlier. He was talking to the Ottesens.'

'Actually,' said Fru Nicolaisen, in that distant, languorous voice, 'actually, he wasn't talking.' Fagermo turned towards her, to find her still gazing at him, apple at her mouth. 'I had to go back, didn't I, Halvard? I left my—'

'Your gloves, you said, dear—'

'That's right, my gloves . . . and he was still there, and the Ottesens were talking with this lecturer in French—what's his name?—and the boy was just sitting there on the other side of the table, looking into his beer.'

'I see,' said Fagermo. 'Did you talk to him at all?'

She looked him straight in the eyes with her deep blue, untrustworthy gaze. 'I said: "Do you happen to have seen a pair of gloves?" ' she said.

That evening Bjørn Korvald, after he had watched the news on his little portable television (the new bankruptcies in Norwegian industry, the terrible plight of Norwegian ship-owners, the allocation of new blocks in the exploitation of North Sea oil) and after he had looked at the list of the evening's programmes (old age pensioners singing age-old songs, and a two-hour programme on the role of women in the emerging Bulgarian trade-union movement of the nineteen-twenties) Bjørn Korvald decided to act on Fagermo's request and drop into the Cardinal's Hat. It seemed the sort of evening when there was nothing much to keep people at home.

It wasn't often that the table where the foreigners usually gathered was empty of an evening. But tonight it was. Quite empty.

CHAPTER 8

TWO GIRLS

In the event, the next day the Trondheim police, through no exertions of their own, came up trumps.

The artist's impression of the dead boy's face had appeared in the Trondheim newspaper that morning, and before ten o'clock a girl had rung up to say she knew who it was.

'She says he's English, and he left Trondheim in the middle of December,' Fagermo's contact in Trondheim said with unjustifiable pride in his voice. 'She hasn't heard from him since. So it looks as if it's the chap you've got there.'

Leaving Tramsø entailed leaving Ekland (who had been assigned to him on the case) in sole charge for a day or more. As a rule, Fagermo contrived to send him out slogging away at some side-issue. Ekland was very adept at sitting in on an interrogation and laboriously taking notes of all the inessentials, but beyond that, and a certain country humour Fagermo liked, he had few talents. It was a wrench to leave things to him, but as Fagermo saw it, the first priority was to fill in the boy's background, and whatever Ekland did while he was away, he could do over again when he came back.

rangement, our living together. Nothing much more than that.'

'And when it stopped being convenient—?'

'We split up, and that was that. No hard feelings, but no particular regrets either.'

'Why exactly did you split up?'

'He just said he'd be away for a bit and wouldn't be coming back to the flat. He may have left his job—I don't know. He'd always been a bit unsure what he was doing for Christmas, then around the middle of December he said he'd be moving out, and I said: "Please yourself." '

'No indication where he was going?'

'He just said north. He didn't give much away as a rule, as I told you. So I just said it seemed a funny time to go north, and left it at that.'

'And since then, nothing?'

'No. I wasn't expecting anything really, though he could have run to a postcard. But then he was dead, wasn't he? But there was something came to the flat for him—at Christmas.'

'Cards?'

'Just one. I kept it for a bit. It was one of those cards with a snapshot of the sender. It was from Åle-sund, and there was an address on the back—Kirkegårdsveien, I think the street was called. He'd had letters from there before, but he'd never said anything about them. This was a girl, with a baby. A kid of a few months, I'd imagine. It just said: "Hope to see you soon. All our love, Anne-Marie and Tor." I didn't keep it.'

'What did you make of it?'

'Well—I thought the kid was probably his.'

Thinking over the interview on the plane to Ålesund, Fagermo found himself most struck by the coolness of the girl. It frightened him, perhaps as all signs of our own ageing frighten us. Even in a small, provincial city like Trondheim the young people had that null sophistication, that terrible chill that reduces all passions and tragedies to a shrug of the shoulders, a muttered remark about 'Just one of those things'. She had lived with the boy and now he was dead, and the experience was hardly more than a flicker of the eyelashes to her. By now she was no doubt living with another man, and soon he would pass out of her life without causing any great flutter of emotion; one day she would contract a marriage as sterile as a hospital operating theatre, and she and her husband would build their own house as soon as possible, aim for a Volvo before they were forty, and bring up two children by the currently accredited text-books.

At Ålesund police station he was given the number of the house in Kirkegårdsveien which seemed to be the one he wanted. He told them he would walk, though they looked at him strangely. Ålesund always affected him badly, and he wanted to get the atmosphere. After Trondheim it was like taking a couple of steps back towards the nineteenth century. A hardfaced city, which only ten years ago had enjoyed the benefits of near-total prohibition, and whose joyless, life-sapping religion seemed to have moulded not just the faces of the older inhabitants, but the stance, the tone of voice, the choice of clothes and colours as well.

At No. 24 the door was opened by a true native

daughter: hardly more than fifty, her hair was dragged back from a pear-shaped, unmade-up face, her mouth pursed into a perpetual line of disapproval and distaste. She was like a heavy autumn mist over the fjord.

'They told me about you,' she said, pulling around her thin body a hideous, coke-grey cardigan. 'You'd better come in.'

She ushered him quickly through the door, held open no more than a fraction, and then shut it quickly. 'It's coming to something,' she said bitterly. 'Police twice in one day.'

Fagermo stood awkwardly in the hallway, enduring her hard stare. 'Did the local man tell you what the business was?' he asked, hoping for a nominal softening.

'Something about a death,' said the woman, tossing her head. 'We've no cause to regret him, if it's true, I can tell you. As you can see for yourself.'

She led the way along the hall to the sitting-room—an airless, lightless room, furnished with hard, high-backed, styleless chairs and a heavy, stained table with dropsical legs, covered with a thick olive-brown cloth.

On one of the chairs, playing disconsolately with a little boy of about a year, was as sad a girl as Fagermo had seen. She was small, but with a fine face—quite unmade up, but regular of feature and with superb, honest eyes. Her hair was cut close, but was of a beautiful shade of auburn which defeated the unflattering attentions it had received, perhaps from her mother. She had clearly been crying, but Fagermo felt that this was only a climax to months of hopeless-

91

ness—to a weight of misery which was part of her family inheritance.

As she stopped playing with it to greet him, the baby let out a howl of outrage.

'*That's* what *he* left behind,' said the woman.

'Mother!' The girl showed signs of bursting into tears again. The woman sat down at the table, contemplating her daughter with a gloomy relish, as if she were personally allocating the wages of sin. It was clear that nothing could be done as long as she was in the room.

'I would like to see your daughter alone,' said Fagermo.

'No, better I'm here too,' said the woman with finality.

'That would be quite impossible,' said Fagermo, with all the firmness he was capable of. He added, untruthfully but convincingly: 'It would be totally against the regulations. We have very strict procedures, you know.'

Like most Norwegians, the woman was cowed by talk of regulations. She got up heavily and moved towards the door.

'You want to watch what she says,' was her parting shot. 'She's a deceitful little hussy.'

She shut the door firmly, but as he was sitting down Fagermo noticed the girl throw an apprehensive glance in its direction.

'Can you carry your little boy?' he asked. 'We could go over by the window and talk.'

A sad half-smile crossed the girl's face. Humping her baby on her arm she went over with Fagermo to the window. He opened it; the air blew chill from the

fjord, but the noise from the traffic would defeat any twitching ears on the other side of the door. The baby gazed rapt on the procession of little boats.

'You're Anne-Marie Lausund—is that right?' Fagermo began.

'Yes.'

'You know that Martin Forsyth is dead?'

'Yes.' The girl's tone was dead, but deliberately damped to stop tears. 'It makes it better in a way. I mean for me. I thought he'd deserted us. Tor and me. Gone on to someone else and just forgotten. I couldn't bear that. Now at least I know that wasn't true—that he would have come back.'

'You wrote to him at Christmas, didn't you?'

'Yes—I sent a card. We didn't write all that often. He rang me up a fair bit—about once a fortnight. And he came down a couple of times from Trondheim.'

'Didn't you do anything when you didn't hear from him?'

'He told me not to. The last time he spoke to me. He rang and said he was taking a holiday from Trondheim. He wouldn't say where, but he said he had something big on. He said he'd contact me as soon as he could—and we'd get married soon. I was so happy—it was the happiest Christmas I've ever had. I expected to hear again so soon—he said we could be married some time in the New Year.'

Two tears forced their way out from the corners of her eyes, and Fagermo imagined the hours of hope deferred, ticking by in this dismal house, making the heart sick.

'How long had you known him?' he asked quickly.

93

'Oh, we met in England, just over two years ago. I was there as an *au pair*.'

'Where did he live?'

'He was living at home. At Mersea, in Essex. It's a small seaside place with a lot of yachting. He'd been around the world a lot, all sorts of places—he seemed to know so much!—and now he was home for a bit. He wasn't happy there, but he liked the work he was doing. It was to do with boats. He loved anything to do with the sea. I was living with some people who worked at Essex University—sociologists. They rather used me, and I wasn't very happy either. So when it was time for me to come home, he came back with me and he got work in Stavanger for one of the North Sea oil companies.They're not so fussy about work permits you know, and he hadn't got one then. He didn't like the work much, but then the permit came through— they let him have one because he was engaged to me, or so we said. So then he left Stavanger, came up to Ålesund for a few weeks, and then got this job in Trondheim.'

'Why didn't he look for work around here?'

Anne-Marie looked at him pityingly. 'We didn't want to stay *here*. Would you? With that sort of atmosphere in the house? And anyway, he wanted to get on, get ahead. He always knew he could get money if he wanted it—he had brains. But to do that you've got to be in a city.'

'So he moved to Trondheim.'

'That's right. And of course by then I was pregnant, so I couldn't go, or he didn't feel I should. He didn't want us to get married until we'd got something to live on and somewhere permanent to live. He said it would be starting off wrong. Of course my parents created merry hell, but he pretended he didn't understand what they were talking about. He was wonderful at letting things just flow over him. He found a flat in Trondheim quite quickly, I don't know how, but he can't have liked the job, I suppose, or else it didn't have the sort of prospects he'd hoped. Because when he phoned at Christmas I assumed he'd decided to move on. I'm sure he had something definite in view this time, and that he intended to call me.'

She said it defiantly, as if this was a bone of contention with her parents.

'I'm sure he did,' Fagermo said.

'He didn't realize, you see, the sort of atmosphere in this house. He had the idea people didn't worry much about illegitimate children in this country. He'd met my mother and father, of course, but he hadn't actually lived in the house. They wouldn't have allowed that, even if we'd wanted it. At that time he didn't know any Norwegian much, and he didn't realize how—how bad they could be. He didn't want us to be married until we could afford it and be really comfortable, and I said I agreed.'

'Did he send you money?'

'I told him not to,' said the girl quickly. 'So we could save. *They* told me I had to get maintenance for Tor from him—they went on and on. Money and the Lord, that's all they think about. Finally I told them I couldn't be sure he was the father . . . That made them worse, of course, but it kept them off that tack.'

'It wasn't true?'

'Oh, of course it wasn't. A great big lie. There's never been anybody else, not since we met.'

'Can you think of anything—' Fagermo paused—
'anything unusual in his past? Perhaps something suspicious, even. Or anything that happened while he
was here—perhaps a quarrel, or a fight with somebody, or something odd? Or could there have been
anything connected with his family?'

'I only met his family two or three times. We went
to pubs on Saturday nights . . . Oh, it's nice, looking
back on it. Before I met him he'd been all over the
place, as I said, and I don't know much about that
part of his life. I used to make him tell me about it—
Greece, Italy, Libya—all the places he'd seen. We used
to sit down near the boats at Mersea, talking about it.
He'd never been in trouble in those years, I'm sure.
He'd have told me. And he never made any enemies
while he was here—except *them*, of course. And no
one can stand *them*. I don't think he even realized—I
mean we'd be talking, or kissing, and they'd be looking at us with hell-fire and damnation in their eyes,
and I just don't think he understood. They don't have
religion much in England.'

'So there's nothing you remember about him that
might suggest any sort of motive for murdering him?'

'Nothing. He was just a nice, ordinary boy. Not ordinary to me, of course. But he wasn't the type to get
murdered, that I'm sure about.'

'But he wanted money. You said that yourself. It's
dangerous to want to make money fast. Do you think
he would have—gone along with anything shady to get
it?'

'He wasn't a crook! He would have earned it! He
had real talent. He always knew he'd do well, but he
didn't need to cheat or steal it.' She paused. 'You're

always hearing these days of people who just take off into nothing. Nothing's heard of them for months, years, and then they come back. They're not crooks—they just live simply.' Fagermo didn't tell her how expensive living simply was these days. 'He was like that. He'd been all over, but he hadn't done anything crooked. He was the type people liked, and he'd always come off well. He was wonderful: so cool and uninvolved. He was the most wonderful thing that will ever happen in my life.'

Fagermo watched for a moment the traffic under the window, and avoided looking at the enthusiastic face beside him. He had his suspicions about Martin Forsyth and his two women. He thought he took the opportunity of the trip to Tomsø to cast himself off from both of them. But of that, nothing could be said. 'What will you do now?' he asked finally, turning back into the room.

'Get out of here. I've been waiting—for him, you know. I always hoped he might ring. And I couldn't trust *them*. I didn't know what they would do if he came, or rang, while I wasn't here. Now I can go, get a job, perhaps study. *Something*, away from here.' She humped her little boy up higher on her arm and turned to see Fagermo to the door. He chucked the baby under the chin.

'I hope he'll grow up like his father,' said Anne-Marie.

CHAPTER 9

NO PLACE

The police at West Mersea regarded Fagermo—emanating, they had been told, from Norway—as a strange bird blown from its accustomed nesting places to land inexplicably on their unlovely marshes. When he told them, in addition, that he was from the far North of the country, from above the Arctic Circle, the information, as it sank in, led them to look at him with the slow country equivalent of curiosity. Even in this age of unaccountable and undesirable migrations, they seemed to feel, nothing like this had been seen there before.

'Cold up there, is it?' said the local police inspector at last, as they sat in the cheerless little station.

'Cold—and hot sometimes, too,' said Fagermo.

'Oh yes? . . . Get a lot of snow, though, I suppose, don't you?'

'Quite a lot,' said Fagermo, refraining from adding that it had buried one of the inspector's fellow townsmen. He had given them no details of the case, and they had showed no curiosity about it.

'We had a Norwegian girl living round here, couple of years ago,' said the inspector, after the obligatory pause. 'One of these *au pairs*' (how he leered), 'name of Anne-Marie.'

'I was talking to her yesterday,' said Fagermo.

'Oh yes?' said the inspector, without surprise, as if Norway to his imagining were about the size of Mersea, and folk could be expected to run into each other almost daily. 'A bit of all right, she was.'

'She wasn't looking too happy yesterday,' said Fagermo. 'How did you meet her?'

'Can't recall now . . . That's right, she used to go with your lad, with that young Forsyth. Met 'em in a pub, with his family. He likes his pint, does Jack Forsyth.' The inspector drew his own hand across his lip, as if in anticipation.

'Is that the father?'

'Aye. He likes his pint, does Jack.' The inspector thought for a bit, as if trying to find something else to say about Jack Forsyth, but he was unsuccessful. 'If you're ready, I'll drive you there,' he said, getting up and feeling for his keys.

They drove the few hundred yards from the station to the Forsyths' house along the boat-strewn quay, then off it towards a collection of depressingly similar houses—a junk-yard of residences put up by a speculative builder, which looked all too likely to have cleared him a packet. Very soon they would have all of the symptoms of age, with none of the dignity.

'It's that one,' said the inspector, pointing. 'Number seventeen. Nice little places, aren't they? Mostly they're retired Londoners live there—we get quite a good type, on the whole. But the Forsyths are local.'

'I see,' said Fagermo, mentally shutting out the hideous estate. 'Did you ever have any trouble with the Forsyth boy?'

'No—there wasn't any trouble from him, that I remember. Wish I could say the same for all the young 'uns round here. All these university students . . . bloody young thugs, most of them. But the Forsyth boy never settled down here, as I remember. He'd be away for a period, then back again for a bit, then suddenly he'd take off. Other than that, we never had any trouble with him.'

'Do the parents know?'

'Oh yes, they know.'

'Did they seem surprised?'

The inspector looked at him in his slow, country way, and scratched his head. 'Can't rightly say,' he drawled meditatively. 'You better talk to them yourself.'

As Fagermo went up the path, through a weedy failure of a garden, he was aware by some sixth sense of inspection from behind the lace curtains of the living-room. Mersea was not so different, after all, from any small Norwegian town, he thought. The curtains fell back into position, and a decorous interval passed between his ring and the opening of the door.

Standing in the opening was a fleshy woman of fifty or so, with tinted auburn hair, carefully made-up face, and hard, gimlet-sharp eyes. She wore a navy Crimplene costume, which seemed odd wear for half past five in the evening. Fagermo wondered if she was going out, if this was in anticipation of his visit, or if it was put on as an attempt at half mourning. It must have been some vague mental image of the last, he decided, because the woman was clearly very unsure how to behave: most notably, she was not sure what she ought to do with her face, though finally she decided she might smile.

'Oh hello-o-o,' she said, in a voice with a sharp country edge like a jagged scythe. 'They told me you'd be coming. Would you like to come in?'

She stood aside, and Fagermo stepped into the hall. She looked up and down the street, and then closed the door and led the way toward the living-room. 'You're from Norway, aren't you?' she said. 'That's nice. I've heard it's very nice there.'

'Yes,' said Fagermo. 'It's very nice.'

'I've heard the countryside is lovely. Mrs Nethercoat down the road went there before it got so dear going abroad, and she said Bergen was lovely.'

'Yes,' said Fagermo. 'It's very lovely.'

They had got themselves to the living-room, and Mrs Forsyth's uncertainty seemed to increase. Some show of emotion seemed to be called for, but she seemed to have no idea of what was appropriate. Her notion of tragedy seemed to date back to Joan Crawford in a forties melodrama, and she gave a convulsive gulp, her hand on her bosom. Then, even she finding this unconvincing, she gave up and contented herself with a careful dab at her eyes.

'Well,' she said, looking at the black-stained handkerchief, 'doesn't do to give way, does it? Will you sit down, Mr—?'

'Fagermo.'

'Oh . . .'

They sat down on two soft, unsteady-looking easy chairs. Tentatively the two of them looked at each other appraisingly. Mrs Forsyth seemed to like what she saw. Fagermo, covertly, did not.

'This must have been a great shock to you,' he said, giving her a cue to display what feelings she had.

'Oh, it *has*,' she said, stretching down toward her heart for an emotion she did not feel. '*Awful*. When they came and told me this morning, I just didn't know what to say!'

Fagermo could believe it. He said: "It was a complete surprise to you?'

'Well, it *was*. Of course it was.' She blinked a dry eye. 'I mean we *heard* from him only—well, let's see, I suppose it would be about last autumn, or not later than summer, anyway. We had a card from him, ever so pretty, one of your towns over there. So of course we didn't think for a moment there was anything wrong . . .'

'He hadn't written to you more recently than that, I suppose—at Christmas, for example?'

'Well, no. But of course Christmas is so *busy* we didn't think anything of it, you know. We've got the other little girl, you see, and it's all *go* then. He wasn't a great writer—we none of us are in this family. Awful when you think of the amount of money they spend on education, isn't it?'

'So usually when he was away, you just got the odd card, is that right?'

'Yes, that's right. Sometimes—you know, when he was away before, and went all over the place—we'd get cards and *I* wouldn't know where they were from. I kept meaning to look them up, but we haven't got an up-to-date atlas.'

She spoke as if towns made a habit of moving restlessly about the world, and she looked at Fagermo as if to establish a sort of intimacy of self-satisfied ignorance. He found her still, as he had from the beginning, oddly repellent.

'You don't have any of the cards, do you?' he asked.

'I don't. I expect I threw away, or gave them to some kiddy or other. They're always doing these *projects* in school these days, aren't they? My little girl or one of her friends is always on at me for this, that, or the other.'

'Do you remember any of the places they came from?'

'Well—' it was clearly a major effort—'I *think* one of them was from Italy. Tripoli or some such town . . . Then there was a town with a funny name—like Aberfan or something, but that's where the kiddies died, isn't it, wasn't it awful? and this one was foreign, I knew from the stamp . . . Anyway, there weren't many cards, no more than two or three to the best of my recollection. And then suddenly he'd turn up on the doorstep, large as life.'

'So you'd say he was a restless boy?'

'Well, they are, aren't they? Young people. I mean, it wasn't like that when *we* were young, was it? 'Course, there was the war, so people had to stay put, but I don't think we *wanted* to go traipsing off to these places the way they do now. I know *I* didn't.'

'But he did?'

'Well, he must have, mustn't he?'

Fagermo was beginning to find this a very strange conversation indeed. As soon as he asked a question about her son, Mrs Forsyth seemed to want to generalize out, to say what 'they' did these days, or to talk about herself—anything, in fact, except talk about her son and his habits. Could it be, Fagermo wondered, that she knew practically nothing about her own son, and had a faint sense of embarrassment at her own blankness?

'You never tried to stop him, though, going off to these "foreign parts"?' he asked.

'Fat lot of use it would have been if I had,' she said shortly. Then, thinking she might have offended him, she added: 'Not that I've anything against foreign countries, of course, and anyway Norway's not really foreign, is it?'

'Not for me,' said Fagermo, and put on a charming smile he usually reserved for worthier recipients. He decided to take the conversation back to an earlier period, when it might be thought she would have been more aware of her son and his doings. He said: 'Had your son been unsettled earlier—when he was at school, for example?'

'Well . . . I wouldn't say that, no. We gave him a very good education . . .'

'You mean he went to private school?'

'Oh no, no. He went to the Grammar School at Colchester. We've still got one, you know.' Her bosom swelled with inexplicable pride.

'Does that mean he won a scholarship?'

'Well, sort of: he got through his eleven-plus. He was never one of the *really* bright ones: they put him in Science. But he always did quite well, really. We let him stay on till he was sixteen, and he got his GCE.'

Fagermo had heard the expression 'Big Deal,' and thought it might be an appropriate reaction to that 'let him stay on'. He asked: 'Was he ever in trouble—girls, for example?'

'Not that I know of. Of course they know so much these days, don't they? Makes you wonder sometimes—the things they come out with. It must be the telly, or some of these set books they read in school. My father would have walloped me, I know that, if he thought I knew half what these youngsters know today. But I don't think Martin was ever in what you'd call trouble.'

'Did he get on with his father?'

'Well . . . I don't know what to say, really. They never *didn't* get on, if you know what I mean . . .'

'No rows?'

'Oh, rows . . . Well, Jack would shout at him now and then, as is only natural, and he'd swear back, but there was nothing . . . nothing *nasty* about it. There wasn't much between them at all, really, if you know what I mean. They both went their own ways.'

Fagermo had a sudden vision of this home as a bare prison, full of self-contained cells—or as a frozen waste of non feeling. Somehow it seemed pointless to continue the conversation, so little did the woman seem to know of what her son was, or thought, or did. He stirred in his chair, preparatory to leaving.

'Did you know your son's Norwegian girl-friend, Anne-Marie Lausund?' he asked.

'Oh *yes*. Ever so nice. So quiet-spoken and that. I *do* think Norwegians are *nice*.' She looked at him invitingly, and was disappointed in his clear blue gaze in return. She chattered on, apparently quite happy to get off the subject of her son. 'Oh yes, we knew her quite well. She came out with us a couple of times, perhaps three. We used to drive over to the Bull at Thaxted, I remember, ever such a nice pub, lots of university people use it, and professional people, and there's ever such a nice atmosphere on Saturday nights. Yes, we had some lovely evenings there. She was such a nice little thing, and spoke lovely English—ever so attractive.'

'She has a baby now.' She looked at him blankly, and Fagermo added: 'Your son's.'

At the thought of grandmotherhood an unconcealable spasm of distaste crossed her face.

'I hope she's not expecting us to do anything about it. We're not well off, and we've got more than enough on our plate as it is. And I mean, you can't *prove* that sort of thing, can you?'

'She's not expecting anything from anybody. I just thought you might be interested.'

'Oh, I see. Well, it's not something anyone'd be proud of, is it? . . . I don't know as I'd want it known.'

'There's no reason why it should be.' They reached the front door, and Fagermo asked: 'Will your husband be in later in the evening?'

'Well, I don't know. He's on the boats, you know. He'll probably be down at the Yachtsman at seven or half past.'

And at half past seven he was, indeed, in the Yachtsman. He was sitting at a table with a group of his pals, engaged in an intense discussion over a newspaper, folded over to the racing results. The landlord pointed him out, and Fagermo took a pint of (he thought) typically weak English beer over to the table, and made himself known. The table fell silent at his name, and he realized that Jack Forsyth had certainly heard the news, and so had his pals.

Forsyth cleared his throat with embarrassment, and then got up and shuffled off with Fagermo to another table, where he sat down and contemplated his beer. His eyes were wetter than his wife's, but not with grief. He searched his mind for something to say, and then finally came out with: 'Rotten thing, this.'

And for the rest of the ten minutes Fagermo stayed, he got out of him nothing more meaningful than that. As he left, he saw him scuttling back to his mates, eager to resume the business of living.

CHAPTER 10

WORK AND PLAY

On the way back from England Fagermo stopped off
again in Trondheim, and took a taxi to the Continental
Shelf Research Institute, where Forsyth had worked.
It was a tubular building on the outskirts of the town,
like a hideous white worm, curiously involuted. Nobody much seemed to be around, or to know where
anybody else was, but finally he found himself talking
to Gunnar Meisal, a large man with a genial, chinny
face that seemed to have been carved out of sand-
stone by an inexpert hand. He at least had known
Forsyth—remembered him from several North Sea expeditions.

'Perfectly capable lad,' he said, sitting Fagermo
down by his desk, piled high with crazy graphs and
endless lines of computer figures. 'Unusually so. A
real find, because they're not so easy to come by these
days. He was experienced, and knew what he was
doing. The great thing was, you didn't have to keep
your eye on him the whole time.'

'He was crew, was he?'

'That's right. The Institute has a couple of boats,
with full time crew, because one or other lot of us

here is out at sea for one reason or another much of the time.'

'Doing what? Or is that top secret?'

'No, no, *what* we're doing isn't top secret, though the details of what we *find* sometimes are.'

'Why?'

'Oil. A lot of what we're doing these days goes straight to the Department of Oil and Energy, or else to the State Oil Company. It's the sort of information that all sorts of foreign oil companies—especially the American and British—would like to get their hands on. The Russians show a lot of interest as well—that's partly why there's been so much Russian activity up in the Northern waters recently: curiously well-equipped fishing-boats—you must know all about that sort of thing, coming from Tromsø.'

Fagermo nodded. It was a common joke how advanced fishing technology had become in Russia. 'Could you give me some idea of what Forsyth was involved in, in his work for you?' he asked.

'Basically it's a question of collecting scientific data: what everyone is interested in is which areas of the North Sea and the Barents Sea are most likely to be profitable. Let me put it very simply—' and Gunnar Meisal crouched forward in an expository pose and gave a little lecture involving gas chromatographs, spectrometers, hydraulic content, multi-channel folds and subsamples. At the end (Fagermo had fixed his eyes on him in desperate attentiveness, and tried to stop them glazing over) Meisal leaned back again in his desk chair, a benevolent expression on his face, conscious of having rendered the subject simple almost beyond the limits of scholarly responsibility. Fagermo trod his way carefully forward with his next question, conscious of the danger of revealing his still near-complete ignorance.

'I see,' he said, sounding unconvincing to himself. 'The long and the short of it is, you're getting information, doing research, that a lot of people—foreign companies, and governments as well—would like to get their hands on.' Meisal nodded. 'Would that be relatively simple information—the sort of thing that can be carried in the head?'

'No, no—certainly not. Highly technical. It's the sort of stuff that we would have to analyse in depth. Or often the Oil and Energy Department uses consultants—highly qualified people in universities, technical colleges, and so forth.'

'So it's difficult to imagine Forsyth being able to make use of the sort of information you might be getting on these trips.'

'Very difficult. Because he'd have to know what he was doing. Much of what we're up to would be quite meaningless to the average crew member; he wouldn't know what was of value, what wasn't. Of course Forsyth was a bright boy, and experienced. It's just *possible*, if he was really clued up, he could get hold of the stuff people are willing to pay good money for. But if it's a question of leaks to foreign concerns, it's much more likely to happen at the consultant level—they would really know what's wanted.'

'And the companies would really pay good money for this information?'

'I wouldn't mind betting. It would have to be good money, to be worth anybody's while. The oil companies have got their fingers in all sorts of pies in this country, since the various North Sea blocks proved workable and profitable. They use some of the same people as the Americans and Russians use—spies, information agents, whatever you like to call them. And they've usually got someone or other on the relevant local councils in their pay: they get a retainer to keep the oil company's interests in mind.'

'*Really?* That could be interesting. Mostly the rightwing people, I suppose?'

Meisal shrugged. 'Not necessarily. The other lot don't go much on oil, but they're pretty fond of money. You know how easy they find it to square things with their consciences. Suddenly you start hearing them say that if there's one thing they think they can justify spending money on it's a bit of extra room for the kiddies to play in, and before you can blink your eyes they've got five-bedroom houses and ten-acre gardens.'

'You could be right,' said Fagermo. 'And of course the oil companies are probably interested in Tromsø.'

'They're interested in all the bigger towns in the North—for when the bonanza starts north of the sixty-second parallel. It'll be this year, or next year—but whenever it is they want to have their lines open well in advance. They say there's even more money to be made from the Northern blocks than there has been from the Southern ones. And they're damn right!'

Fagermo sat for a moment in thought. 'Well, well,' he said finally. 'The modern gold rush. It seems to have some funny side-effects . . . Now, this boy, Forsyth, did he strike you as trustworthy?'

Meisal pondered. 'It's not something we think about: security is something that usually only matters higher up, and anyway the cloak-and-dagger aspects are not really our affair, only the research . . . I was just with him on a couple of trips. He was certainly a pleasant chap: not talkative, but you could talk *to* him. He fitted in well, even though he didn't talk much Norwegian. He liked earning money—from overtime, that sort of thing—but most of the crew-men do. And I knew we wouldn't keep him for long, because he was too bright. There are lots of jobs waiting for a chap like that. I imagine he was biding his time, saving up, and he just moved on when he was ready.'

'So you weren't surprised when he left? Did he actually give in his notice?'

'I imagine so, though you never know with crew: they can be pretty casual. Would you like me to find out?'

'Can you?'

Meisal took up the phone and dialed a number: 'Kjell—you remember that Forsyth boy, on the boat? Did he give in his notice before he left? . . . Just took off . . . No hint at all? . . . When was this? . . . I see, thanks . . . Not the immigration people, the police . . . He's dead.'

He put down the phone.

'He left without giving notice just before Christmas, and never came back.'

'The last part I know already,' said Fagermo. 'Well, I'm grateful to you for your help.' He got up to go, but paused at the door. 'You've not given me much idea of the boy's personality. Did you know him well enough to get one? Did he make any impression on you at all?'

Meisal thought, his Grand Canyon face resting on

his cupped hands: 'Self-contained . . . self-reliant . . . ruthless . . .'

'Why ruthless?'

'You asked for impressions. That was mine. You don't get much opportunity to be ruthless in the middle of the North Sea on a geological research expedition. But that's how he struck me. Someone who knew what he wanted, and went after it.'

Back in Tromsø, Fagermo went straight to the station in the setting sun of early evening and caught up with developments. Sergeant Ekland was off duty, and even now (no doubt) was snoring in front of his television set with a beer-glass in his hand. He had left behind a report of very much the kind which Fagermo had anticipated: written in a Norwegian which (even granted the chaotic free-for-all which is the current state of the language) could only be described as semi-literate, it detailed the various approaches by members of the public to the police following publication of the artist's impression of the dead boy in the local paper two days before. Reading through the details as mistyped by Ekland, Fagermo could only feel that there was more to be said for literacy than was usually allowed these days—and for typing lessons for policemen as well.

Among the disorganized mass of details and names and addresses there was one item that caught his eye. Among others who said they had seen him (but, as far as could be judged from Ekland's notes, had had nothing whatsoever more to say about him) was a Fru Barstad who manned a kiosk up in Biskopsgate as it wound up from the main street towards the top of the

113

island. Ekland had noted down the date she gave—December 20—but beyond that his notes consisted entirely of irrelevancies: her marital status (widow); her age (sixty-five); the number of years she had worked at the kiosk (twenty-five). But Fagermo did not need to be told how long Fru Barstad had worked at the kiosk. He had known Fru Barstad from her first days there. On an impulse he put on his coat and went out into the street.

When Elin Barstad had begun to work at the kiosk in Biskopsgate she was a capable woman of forty whose husband had begun to take the easy way out of marriage to her and was graduating to full-time alcoholism. Fagermo had not yet even begun at *gumnas*. She had sold him chocolates, mild pornography and his first cigarettes. Over the years the pornography on offer had got less mild, but Fagermo had lost the need for it. For old times' sake, though, he still bought chocolates or cigarettes there, if he was in the vicinity. And as he had grown into a young-looking middle-aged policeman with an amused mouth and sharp eyes, Fru Barstad had aged into the kind of old lady Norway alone can produce—the kind of old lady who is convinced she is the backbone of Norway. Bulky, upright, tougher than any man, she was a heavyweight opponent, and took on all comers. At sales or crushes of any kind her umbrella, wielded vigorously, felled all bystanders and brought her to the front of the queue, where her voice, first cousin to Kirsten Flagstad's without the musicality, summoned the shop assistant to her immediate service. She was tough, pushing, opinionated, aggravating and totally irresistible, a force of nature that the most foul-mouthed teenager or drunken tramp could never hope to best. She sat in her kiosk like Pius IX in the Vatican, ruling her roost and the streets around, utterly secure in her own infallibility. She made no concessions to manners, good-nature or old acquaintanceship. She simply *was*.

'Yes?' she enunciated sourly, when Fagermo had stood patiently before her counter for something approaching a minute.

'I'll have a bar of chocolate,' he said. She handed it to him silently, took his money, and slapped it into the till.

'I hear you've been giving us some valuable information,' said Fagermo conversationally. Fru Barstad sniffed virtuously, as if to say: I did my duty.

'Mind if I ask you a few more questions?'

A smile of triumph wafted over Fru Barstad's face. 'I knew that chap didn't know his job! I said to myself: those are stupid questions you're asking, and you're forgetting to ask the right ones! But it wasn't *my* business to teach him his job!' She sniffed again. She took great pleasure in the inferiority and moral frailness of the world in general. Fagermo saw no reason to take up the cudgels for Sergeant Ekland's intelligence. No policeman likes lost causes.

'How can you be sure it's the same boy?' he asked.

'Well, of course I can't, and I'm not. I said so to him. These artist's impressions—they're very clever, but they're not like a photo, are they?'

'We could show you the body,' said Fagermo. A definite flicker of interest passed over Fru Barstad's face.

'That's as you please. Anyway, as I told your little I-should-be-on-TV sergeant, I know most of the customers at this kiosk by this time. Most of them live around here—or they wander up after the pictures.' She surveyed gloomily the white road shading into darkness as it wound down to the town. 'And there's not much I don't know about *some* of them that come here, I can tell you! Don't give me you're police, because police don't know half of it! So anyway, when there *is* someone completely new, and in the middle of winter to boot, you notice them.'

'I suppose you do,' said Fagermo, who believed her. 'But the date—I don't see how you can be so sure of *that*.'

'Ah, but I can!' said Fru Barstad, with gloomy triumph. 'Because it was my last night on before Christmas. I'd ordered a taxi to take me to the airport, because my sister was coming up on the night plane from Bodø to stay with me for Christmas—and a right foolish idea *that* turned out to be! Anyway, I was just thinking of locking up for the night when he came along and demanded a hot dog or something, I forget what. I muttered a bit, but I could hear he was English—'

'You're sure about that?'

'You think I could have been here twenty-five years without being able to hear whether someone's English or not? We used to have hundreds and hundreds here every summer, before they got their Troubles.'

'That makes it pretty certain it was Forsyth you saw, then.'

'Anyway, I got it for him, whatever it was, and then I locked up. Then, when the taxi came, we drove to the airport, and I saw him again, just up the road here—' she nodded her head up the road, along the way that led over the crown of the island to the air-

116

port—'there he was finishing his hot dog and standing talking to someone, and I thought to myself: Well, you are a fast one, and no mistake.'

'What do you mean? Was it a woman?'

'Of course it was a woman. He was talking to her by the roadside as if he'd just picked her up—or her him, you can't tell these days.' She sniffed vigorously, a testimony that she was brought up in the days when men were men and women were women, and the ritual dance was danced with quite other steps.

'This is interesting,' said Fagermo. 'If you're right about the date this was only his second night here.'

'This town,' said Fru Barstad darkly.

'Was it someone you knew, this woman? One of the usual?'

'Oh no—though I think I've seen her before. Definitely from Tromsø or around, I'd say. *Looked* quite respectable. Smart, permed hair, took care of herself. Oh no, definitely not one of the regulars.'

'Could you describe her, or recognize her again?'

'Not to swear to—I only saw her in the headlights. She was a blonde: twenty-five, thirty, thirty-five—these days you can't tell, not like you could thirty years ago. Good-looking, well-dressed—there's nothing that stands out about her that I remember.'

'Just thinking back to how they looked,' said Fagermo carefully, 'would you say they were meeting by appointment, or just casually?'

Fru Barstad considered the question carefully, gazing up into the darkness. 'Well, as I said, my impression was that one had picked the other up, and I dare say there was something that made me think that—I'm not one for jumping to conclusions without I have my reasons. It's the way people stand, isn't it? I mean, not too close, trying to look casual, sizing each other up. It's like dogs, isn't it? And it usually ends up pretty much the same way, too!'

Fagermo sighed. 'It's a pity. If it was just something casual, like asking the way, it probably led to nothing. But the boy did get in late that night, and it would have been interesting if he'd met this woman by appointment.'

'Well, he wouldn't have been just asking her the way somewhere, you can bank on that,' said Fru Barstad. 'If he'd wanted to know that, he'd have asked me. People do all the time—it's more likely I'd know than someone you stop casually in the street.'

'She may have stopped him.'

'But I *think* she's local. And he didn't look in the least Norwegian, in spite of being fair.'

'Do you think she lives around here?'

'No—I'd have seen her more often. But there are people you just see occasionally—walking home after the last bus has gone, or out for their Sunday stroll. She's one of them.'

'She may have just asked him the time,' said Fagermo despondently. But Fru Barstad was not willing to have her information disregarded as easily as that.

'Very likely she did ask him the time,' she said, with her lips pursed. 'It's been done before! But it didn't stop at that. The lights were on them as we drove up the hill, and when we passed them they were *talking*. You don't talk when somebody asks you the time, unless you're hoping it will lead to something else.'

'You could be right,' said Fagermo.

'There's no "could be" about it,' she returned

sharply. 'No doubt you smart boys in the police think you know better than the rest of us, but you parade around in your uniforms and people make themselves scarce when they see you coming. You don't see half of what's going on. Do you know what this job has made me?'

A cantankerous old battle-axe, thought Fagermo to himself, but he merely raised his eyebrows.

'A student of human nature. You look at the way people walk, the way they hold their hats, the way they get into their cars, and you can tell what they're up to, or what's about to happen to *them*.'

'You didn't by any chance guess the young man was about to be murdered, I suppose?' murmured Fagermo.

'Not that. Of course not. But I'll tell you this. When I saw him in the headlights, he was thinking of bed. And it wasn't his own!'

CHAPTER 11

MARITAL RELATIONS

'That's funny,' said Sergeant Ekland, with an expression of sublime complacency on his face. 'Aren't women funny. She never said anything about that to me.'

'No,' said Fagermo, with equal complacency.

It was the next morning, and Ekland was sitting in Fagermo's office—massive, self-congratulatory and elegantly lethargic. He had the happy knack of never being able to see that he had done wrong, or done too little, or might have done better. He had the equally happy knack of giving to everything he did an equal amount of attention or inattention: knocking up a shelf in the garage or investigating a murder case occupied in his mind places of equal importance or unimportance, and were accordingly done in much the same take-it-or-leave-it manner. Such men live to a ripe and inconvenient old age.

'Well anyway, now we have a woman in the case,' said Fagermo. 'Which would at least have the effect of brightening it up, except that it's a totally unknown woman.'

'What about that Professor's wife you were talking about?' asked Ekland. 'The one you said was the nymphet type? Couldn't it be her? You said she was blonde.'

'Oh she was, along with fifty percent of this town. I suppose she's about twenty-five, though she looks a lot younger. There's no reason to think it's her rather than anybody else, though. She'd be a long way from home—she lives on the mainland.'

'Some things are best done a long way from home,' said Sergeant Ekland sagely. 'I'd follow it up if I were you. As a matter of fact, I think I've heard of her before.'

'Really?'

'The boys did a raid at the students' place a few months ago—drugs—and I have an idea she was one of the people there. Wife of one of the professors, but more of an age to be a student. Can't be many of them.'

'I don't know about that. I have the impression that's a bit of an occupational hazard. Did you say drugs? That could be interesting. Was she brought in?'

'Well, actually it wasn't drugs. They went through the place with a toothcomb, but there wasn't a trace. It must have been some kind of hoax—they had a tip-off by telephone, and that evening the students did something else: had a demonstration about something, or blew something up, I forget what. All they found was a nice sexy party with nothing worse than alcohol. They were all students there except her.'

'So she sort of stood out, did she? Was it really a sexy party, or are you making that up?'

'Would I?' asked Ekland, injured. 'There were ten or twelve there, mostly men, nobody had a stitch on, all the furniture had been moved out and there were mattresses all over the floor. By the time our boys had finished the investigation they were down to their underpants themselves. Just my luck I wasn't on duty! But there were no drugs.'

'Well, well, just an ordinary student party, eh? I wonder if she goes in for that sort of thing often. When I saw her she certainly seemed—well, never mind. Where she met the boy—if it was her—is only five or ten minutes from Prestvann Student Hostel. She could have been entertaining herself for the evening.'

'She's probably not important,' said Ekland lazily, the flicker of interest, or lust, he had shown now being replaced by his habitual lethargy. 'I mean, the guy probably just slept with her. We've no evidence she goes around killing the blokes she sleeps with—otherwise the student hostel would have been littered with corpses that night.'

Fagermo spread out his hands in a gesture of helplessness.

'What can we do but follow up all the contacts he had while he was in Tromsø? We have precious little else, though of course I'm thinking what I can do about tracking him further in the past. Meanwhile, we're bound to probe his connection with the people he met here, like this woman. Did he know her from before? Did they meet by arrangement? Did he tell her anything about what he was doing here? That sort of thing.'

'Doesn't sound particularly hopeful to me,' said Ekland with a big sigh.

'It's not. But they're possibilities, and they're about

all we've got at the moment . . .' He paused, and looked down again at the jungle of Ekland's notes. 'I suppose one of the things we could begin to do would be to draw up a timetable of his activities while he was in Tromsø.'

He took up a clean sheet of paper.

'Let's see. He arrives some time during the morning of the nineteenth, probably tries various hotels, and then lands up at Tromsø's Little Hilton—Botilsrud's Pensjonat. We don't know what he did for the rest of the day, but in the evening—almost the entire evening—he was in the Cardinal's Hat. Slept at the Pensjonat. Next day is pretty blank, but we have a reliable sighting around ten o'clock at night, an encounter with a woman, and then a late arrival back at the Pensjonat—around three o'clock or so.'

Fagermo paused: 'Question: if he was sleeping with the woman, why go back to the Pensjonat at all? It can't have been just to get his money's worth.'

'Husband?' hazarded Ekland, with a lazy, experienced air.

'Not many jobs where you knock off around two or three in the morning.' Fagermo pulled the paper towards him again. 'Next day, it seems probable, he was killed. Where? Possibly over there on the mainland, though he could just as easily have been taken there by car. The doctors say he *was* moved after death. When was he killed? Any time after dark, if it was outside—in any case, it was dark practically all day . . . I see you've got a sighting for him around midday, day unspecified.' He peered down at Ekland's notes trying to find something more concrete, and Ekland leaned forward too with an apparently quite disinterested curiosity. 'Seems to be someone called Solheim. Is that right? Who was he? Reliable?'

'Oh yeah,' said Ekland, with false confidence. 'Some fairly high-up bod in the Post Office. Said he saw him in the Viking Café a bit after midday.'

'Anything else?'

Ekland scratched his head. 'Not that I remember.'

Fagermo, getting that haloed feeling one does get when keeping one's good humour in circumstances guaranteed to enrage the average Archangel, pulled the phone towards him and got on to the central switchboard at the Post Office.

Solheim, he learned, was a fairly big wig with a ridiculously long title that could mean anything. When he came on the line he sounded competent and decided. He often went to the Viking Café, just by the Post Office, when he forgot to bring his lunch sandwiches. He remembered the boy because it was just before Christmas, and you didn't see many tourists around that time. He couldn't remember the exact date, but there were lots of people with Christmas packages. He had picked out the boy as English from his clothes. He said a few words to him because he liked talking English now and then—having been there in the war.

'What sort of thing did you say?'

'Well, I think I asked him if he needed any help—he was poring over a map.'

'Did he accept the offer?' asked Fagermo, his hopes rising.

'No, he didn't. He seemed sort of—reserved. He wasn't exactly rude, but he didn't seem to want to talk, you know how it is. So I just went on to another table.'

'You say he was poring over a map. Do you remember what sort it was? A motorist's map?'

'No, no: it was a map of the town—you know the one: it's the only big one available, with all the streets on.'

'Did you by any chance notice where he was looking? Somewhere on the island?'

There was a pause. 'Now you come to mention it, I think I do remember. He'd had to fold it—it was too big for the table. He was looking at the bottom section, the mainland—bottom lefthand corner, in fact. That's where his finger was.'

'Good, that's very useful. Did you notice him again?'

'I think he went out not long after that.'

'And you can't swear to the day—that's a pity.'

'No, I wouldn't swear to a date, because you just don't remember things like that. But it was certainly just before Christmas . . . and it was probably a Friday.'

'Probably Friday?' said Fagermo, flicking through the last year's desk calendar he still had in his drawer.

'Yes: it's mostly Friday I forget my sandwiches. That's the day my wife goes to work early, and she's not there to remind me to take them.'

'I'm very, very grateful to you,' said Fagermo, putting down the phone. He pulled towards him the sheet on which he had detailed the boy's movements, and entered: '12.00 Viking Café? About to go over to the mainland?' He sat back.

'I wouldn't mind betting,' he said, 'that he was killed not far from where he was found. Anton Jakobsensvei, Isbjørnvei—one of those around there. They're on the bottom lefthand end of the map . . .' He looked again at his little timetable of the boy's movements. 'There's still an awful lot of blank spaces. A lot of time unaccounted for.'

'Isbjørnvei,' said Sergeant Ekland, who throughout the telephone conversation had been picking his teeth with an intentness and concentration he rarely exhibited in his day-to-day work, and had now reached an excavation of particular delicacy and interest. 'Isn't that where the Prof lives—the one with the dishy wife?'

'Yes,' said Fagermo with a sigh. Trust Ekland to notice the blindingly obvious. Still, when there were so few promising lines of investigation, the obvious could certainly not be ignored. Sergeant Ekland, having finished the hideous probings, was grinning like a manic model.

'Oh, stop posing, man—drive me there,' snapped Fagermo.

Outside the station, as they got into their car, Fagermo said: 'Wait a sec. Drive me over to Brennbygget first—that's where the Prof works. There's no point in talking to the girl if the husband's there. I've done that already.'

They drove past the Amundsen statue and the little customs shed, and came to the office block which temporarily housed the library and various other parts of the university. Fagermo pottered up the stairs, looking into the library and the canteen, outside which the various left-wing student groups fought out their ideological battles in shrill red wall posters dotted with exclamation marks. On the fourth floor he found the Department of Languages and Literature, and here he met a snag: he was just about to enquire at the office whether Professor Nicolaisen was teaching today when he saw him stalking along the corridor towards the dark, smelly little seminar room, set windowless in the middle of the building. Nicolaisen saw him, stopped, and regarded him with a commendably frank dislike. Since he made no opening to start even the most casual of conversations, Fagermo was forced to accept that the onus was on him.

'Oh, Professor Nicolaisen—I wondered if you were teaching at this hour.'

'I am. My students are waiting,' said Nicolaisen, nodding towards the seminar room where one or two students were sprawled in attitudes not notably expressive of anticipation.

'Oh, then I won't keep you,' said Fagermo. 'I just wanted—' he nearly dried up for a moment, but invention seldom failed him entirely and he seized gratefully on the first thought that happened to come into his head: 'I just wanted to know if you remembered whether Martin Forsyth was wearing a ring of any sort when you met him in the Cardinal's Hat.'

Nicolaisen's face, creviced like a relief map of his native country, expressed as clearly as words: what a foolish question! He said: 'Good heavens, how could I be expected to remember that! It's not the sort of thing one notices.'

'Well, well,' said Fagermo, glad to make his getaway so easily, 'that's all I wanted to ask. Perhaps somebody else will have noticed.'

'Not many Englishmen do wear wedding-rings,' said

127

Nicolaisen, to his departing form. He loved imparting useless information, and now went on to do more of it to his seminar group, in the sort of mood that guaranteed that withering and crushing would be the order of the day.

On the drive out to Isbjørnvei and the Nicolaisens' residence Fagermo remembered why the question of the ring had flashed into his mind. The boy had been wearing one, presumably, when he died: the rounded indentation was there on the fourth finger of his right hand. Nicolaisen's reaction had been interesting . . . A possibility of further questioning suggested itself.

When they got to Isbjørnvei Fagermo tossed up in his mind the advantages of leaving Ekland outside and taking him in with him. Finally he decided on the latter: he had a certain dreadful appeal which might go straight to the heart, or something, of Fru Nicolaisen. Together they clambered over unswept snow, watched by an unashamedly interested face from the kitchen window. The response to the ring on the doorbell was immediate—even, one might have fancied, enthusiastic. Fru Nicolaisen came tripping downstairs and pulled open the door invitingly.

'I knew you'd come back,' she said. 'Oh—you've brought a friend with you.'

It was one way of putting it. Ekland brightened up visibly and took a vital interest in his official duties for the first time since the case began. Fru Nicolaisen was wearing something between a brunch coat and a brunch jacket—a short, frizzy, nylon-gauzy creation that led one to wonder if she was wearing anything underneath and kept one within an ace of finding out. Fagermo generously allowed Ekland to follow her upstairs. She sat them down on the sofa and then, without asking, went into the kitchen, opened a bottle of beer, and poured three glasses.

'Isn't this cosy?' she said, looking from one to the other with experienced naivety.

'We actually came to ask you some more questions, Fru Nicolaisen,' said Fagermo.

'Lise, call me Lise,' said Fru Nicolaisen; and then, with a pretty pout: 'But why shouldn't we be comfortable? So much nicer to relax. Especially as I suppose these are the questions you didn't like to ask while my husband was around . . .'

'Well, that's pretty much the truth,' admitted Fagermo. Then, chancing his arm, he added: 'Or anyway, ones we thought you might not have been quite honest in answering.'

She put on an enigmatic smile, then let it fade slowly, fascinatingly from her face.

'Did you notice whether Martin Forsyth was wearing a ring when you met him at the Cardinal's Hat?' Fagermo asked experimentally.

Lise Nicolaisen raised her pretty blonde-grey eyebrows and stared at him: 'What an odd question. I was hoping for something more . . . personal. Yes, he wore a ring—do you mean specifically when he was in the Cardinal's Hat that night, or just generally?'

'Well—'

'Though actually I did notice when I met him the first time, because it's one of the things one *does* notice, or I do, anyway. Not that it makes much difference to the way they behave, sometimes.'

'So you met Martin Forsyth more than once?'

'I *always* meet attractive men more than once,' said

Lise Nicolaisen, with a baby-doll wriggle of her shoulder, and that wicked pout. 'That's why I knew you'd come back!' She curled her legs up under her on the chair opposite them and looked even more like something out of a 'fifties film. Sergeant Ekland's note-taking ceased entirely as he took in the augmented expanses of thigh.

'So you met him again—at around ten o'clock the next night?' hazarded Fagermo. She opened her adorable eyes still wider.

'At ten o'clock the next *morning*, actually,' she said with a little giggle. 'Still, it was a good try.'

'Ten o'clock next *morning*?' said Fagermo, disconcerted. 'Then you didn't meet him on the evening of the twentieth up Biskopsvei?'

'No. Why? Did someone? He *does* seem to have got around, doesn't he? I'm sure I got the best out of him.'

Fagermo tried to readjust his ideas. Was she telling the truth? Why should she admit to the morning but deny the evening? He said: 'So you met him in the morning. Here?'

'No, actually not here. I don't often—unless it's one of my husband's students. It—excites them, you know, sometimes. It doesn't bother me particularly. There are some who like to keep things within the Department, but I'm not one of them. It seems silly to me. I like to range around!'

'Where did you meet?'

'Up in the student hostel in Prestvannet. It's a friend's room. He got me a duplicate key, and I use it in daytime now and then, when he's at lectures. Do you know, none of the hotels in this town will let rooms by the hour!'

'How did you manage to arrange all this? You didn't have much time.'

She giggled cosily and sipped her beer. 'Who needs time? I don't. I have talking eyes.' She looked at Sergeant Ekland and blinked invitingly. 'Did you notice I had talking eyes? . . . So had he. We agreed to it when I was collecting my husband, actually, though we didn't say a word. Then, when I went back for my gloves I just whispered the place and time, and he nodded. It's awfully simple to do, Inspector, if you've got my experience.'

'I'm sure,' said Fagermo. 'And when you met you—?'

'That's right. Do you want details, Inspector, or have you read the little manuals?'

'Hgghh-hmmm. Er, did you talk as well?'

She considered. 'I can't remember. I expect I made coffee. We may have talked a bit while we drank it. Yes—that's right. He said he'd been on some sort of boat in Trondheim, mentioned some of the expeditions they'd been on. Sounded deadly boring, all male and all that, but I think it was scientific or something.'

'Anything else?'

She threw back her head. 'Let's see. What's the usual? I expect I asked how long he would be in Tromsø—that's right, I did—and he said he didn't know for sure, but he hoped to finish his business the next day, and if he did he'd probably take the plane the day after.'

'Back to Trondheim?'

'I suppose so. I don't remember.'

'Anything else?'

'I don't think so. There wasn't much time . . . I

don't go in for too much talking. That's the trouble with half the university people: it's all jabber and no—'

'And you parted—when?'

'Parted! Sounds like a novelette! I suppose we left the flat about half past eleven. When we walked down to town it was light. We "parted" in the main street.'

'Did he say where he was going, or anything?'

'No. I think he just said "Thanks".' She looked at him wonderingly. 'He was a man of few words.'

'I see,' said Fagermo. 'Well—at least that fills in one of my blank spots in the timetable I'm making of his movements. I suppose there's nothing else you'd like to tell me about him?'

She giggled sexily and said in a Joan Greenwood voice: 'No . . .'

Fagermo sighed, drained his beer and got up. 'Well, I'm very grateful to you—'

'Funny to think of him buried up there . . . all stiff,' said Lise Nicolaisen, who seemed to feel no compulsion to hide her more appalling thoughts. 'When I slept with him just a day or two before. Sort of—exciting, somehow!'

'If you should think of anything else—'

'I'll come along to the police station,' she said, unwinding herself from her chair and putting on a pretty pout of anticipation. 'I've always wanted to.'

Fagermo let Ekland go first down the stairs, but at the bottom he turned, received a very full view of what Fru Nicolaisen was not wearing under her brunch coat, and—swallowing his embarrassment, which she seemed to find charmingly old-fashioned—he said: 'You are quite sure you didn't meet him again in the evening?'

'Absolutely sure,' said Lise Nicolaisen. 'Have I hidden anything from you?' Fagermo spluttered. 'I had another date, as far as I remember. It wasn't with Amnesty International, so it may have been the Warm Clothes For the Elderly Committee, or Reclaiming the Alcoholics. I'm chock-a-block full of good works, Inspector!'

Fagermo gained the front door and slipped and slithered down to the car. Ekland already had his hand on the driver's door, but as Fagermo climbed in he said: 'Oh, I've forgotten my gloves,' and made his way nippily back to the front door.

Christ, thought Fagermo, settling grumpily into the passenger seat. How bloody uninventive. Gloves.

CHAPTER 12

ONE DAY

As March shaded into April, the elements played coy games with the North Norwegians. Some days they flattered them with hopes of an early spring: the roads were clear, and there was the pleasure of walking on nature's own tarmac again; sometimes the temperatures rose above zero, and on some evenings, as the sun set in a clear sky, the surrounding hills seemed draped with pink snow, like enormous cheap cakes. These were the days of delusion. Next day the skies would be angry grey and lowering, the snow would fall, and by nightfall nature white in tooth and claw had reasserted its accustomed iron rule.

It was on one of the flirtatious days, when the town and the surrounding fjords and mountains were bathed in blinding sunlight reflected from the snow, that the people who had briefly met Martin Forsyth back in December had cause to remember him again. It was nearly two weeks since the body had been found, and already the newspapers had gone on to other things—contenting themselves with brief remarks about the Inspector in charge being in touch with Interpol, and vague suggestions that the body being found in Tromsø was totally fortuitous.

Fagermo was content to leave that suggestion in the air. The apparent dearth of interest in the case, however, did not reassure all the people who had crossed Forsyth's path during that fatal visit. More than one wondered exactly what the wider implications of the murder were, and whether there would be any fall-out that might involve others. And one of those persons was still very worried.

So as they went about their daily business, many of them thought about Martin Forsyth.

Professor Nicolaisen travelled to work by car on those days when his wife did not require it for her private purpoess. He parked it behind the Post Office, getting tetchy if there was a lack of space. The morning was, for Professor Nicolaisen, a process of gathering tetchiness. He would have been disappointed if there had been nothing to thwart or aggravate him, but fortunately there always was. Today, as usual, the lift was out of order. He sighed theatrically at nobody in particular, and trudged up the bleak coal-grey stairs, telling himself how bad it was for his heart—though physically that organ was in perfect working order.

He pushed open the main door on the fourth floor and went into the bright orange, blue and white corridors of the Department of Languages and Literature. It seemed to please him no better than the dreary stairs. His nose twitched. The air was redolent of aborted research and stale feminism. He went to the common-room to collect his mail, throwing grunts in the direction of the newspaper readers there. In his pigeonhole was a pay-slip for external examining: four-fifths to the government, one-fifth to himself. His lip curled, and he emitted a sound like an outraged cockerel.

So far the morning was going well.

Those who knew Professor Nicolaisen well—and really, in a small university, there was not much option—contended that it was best to get hold of him early on. Something got into him as the day wore on—'home thoughts', said some wit who knew how his wife spent her time. Or perhaps it was just the cumulative effect of contact with his kind. Certainly the coffee-break at twelve seemed to do nothing for his humour, perhaps because most of the others in the coffee rooms were so much younger than himself, perhaps because of the radical orthodoxies they spouted. Whatever the cause, he was best left alone after the sun had started its long, lingering decline.

Which was bad luck for the student who sat in his room at two-fifteen presenting to his professor the plan for his forthcoming thesis on Crime as Social Protest in the Works of Arthur Morrison. It could not be the chosen author that was niggling Nicolaisen, because he had never heard of him. It could not be the proposed organization of the thesis, because he was not listening. He sat in his poky room, surrounded by cheap reproductions of Gainsborough and Stubbs, and looked witheringly at the boy as he sat reading painstakingly from his disquisition.

Jeans. Check shirt covering grubby sweat-shirt. Fair hair, and the lightest of stubbles on his chin and cheeks. Halvard Nicolaisen's eyes were odd, neither attentive nor abstracted, clearly not listening, and yet *noticing*. Thoughts of some kind were clearly going through his brain, for he sometimes swallowed in a meaningful way that ended up in a little whinny. The student would half look up, then return hastily to his notes.

Jeans. Long thin body. Fair hair. Nicolaisen snuffled. It was that that reminded him . . . reminded him of . . . He pulled himself together. Silly to give way. Nothing to do with *this* boy. Incredibly silly to give way . . .

'Then I thought to give a whole chapter to *The Hole in the Wall*, concentrating on the East End background and taking up the whole subject of the derivation from *Our Mutual Friend*—'

He reminds me . . . There's a look there . . . Fair hair. Check shirt. Professor Nicolaisen emitted a choking sound that threatened explosion:

'Oh Christ in hell, get out of my office, you incompetent driveller,' he said, to one of his more promising honours students.

Nan Bryson sat in a dusty corner of the little US Information Office, copy-typing busily and thinking—for she was competent enough to do both, though any demand for original endeavour found her faintly lacking. She always worked enthusiastically, because her job with the Office was important to her: it was her lifeline, her means of staying put in Tromsø. Here she had put down some feeble roots, got herself into some kind of circle. Nowhere in the States did she have either. If she nursed feelings of having been rejected at an early age she did so for the excellent reason that she had been rejected at an early age.

What Nan was typing was not of any great interest, to her or very probably to anyone else. She was producing paperwork for the bureaucratic machine that in its turn could be expected to beget more such. If the Information Office was indeed part of the ludicrously ineffective CIA network, it kept its secrets from her. She was always telling people that, and never being believed. Perhaps she didn't entirely want to be believed. Perhaps something did go on here that was vital to the security of the Free World. Perhaps her boss, dark and bulky, hunched over something behind his desk, was reading some sort of secret report. But it looked more like a paperback.

She wondered why spying was on her mind. Was she afraid she was being investigated herself? Fat lot they'd find. No—that's right: they'd been talking about it in the SAS pub the other night, all the local drunks and near-drunks. They'd got hold of a rumour that the dead boy was a spy. Charlie Brown she thought of him as, Martin Forsyth she now knew his name was. The gossip was that he was a spy. She'd sat for a couple of hours over her beer just to listen to the talk. As usual in that kind of place it got progressively wilder and wilder. From being frankly and openly gossip, it became by the minute more and more bogusly 'inside'.

And yet—what if he had been? What if he'd scraped acquaintance with her because he had found out she worked at the Information Office? She did not stop to examine whether he had scraped acquaintance with her, or she with him. Nor even whether the thought was flattering. It was a story, a dream, a web of possibility in which she sat at the centre. Bunched over her typewriter, tapping out a long and heavily reasoned memorandum about the proposed closing down of the

Information Office's unused library, she set up an image of herself being courted by glamorous male spies in the pay of foreign leftist governments, and her pale, uninteresting little face lit up.

She preened herself.

In his room in the Faculty of Science, Dougal Mackenzie stood looking out over the fjord. The water sparkled, small fishing boats chugged up and down, there was much activity. He could see over to where his own little boat, new and almost unused, was moored. Turning his head he could see towards Hungeren, the rows of houses, the mountains . . .

He had his dog with him today. Scenting restlessness, and scenting some possible advantage to himself, Jingle had got up from the rig by the door and tentatively come over, looking up pleadingly, wagging his tail, and panting slightly. Looking down at him, Dougal Mackenzie remembered him barking in the snow, tugging at the ear, remembered the gradual uncovering of that young human face.

Quite suddenly, he retched.

Business was slack in Ottesen's men's outfitters when Fru Ottesen dropped in on her husband in the course of the morning's shopping. Two assistants were draped over a rail of sports jackets discussing the English FA Cup match on Saturday's television. Helge Ottesen was sitting in his little office at the back, working on sums that never seemed to come right.

'Not much doing today,' said Gladys Ottesen cheerily.

Her husband grunted. 'Not much doing any day

these days. It's these damned package tours to Britain. They ought to be banned. Three hours in Oxford Street and they buy up clothes to last them for years. It's ruining the Norwegian clothing industry.'

'Well, it won't last,' said his wife, with her usual optimism. 'Prices are going up in Britain too. There's not the saving there was, everybody's saying it. And you don't get the quality.'

'If only people *did* realize it,' said Helge Ottesen dubiously.

'Oh, they will, they will,' said his wife. 'I've got a lovely bit of cod for your *middag* . . .'

But after his wife had gone Helge Ottesen went back to his figures and sank further and further into despondency. If Gladys did but know, things were pretty grim. Or would be if it weren't for that little extra, that delicious untaxed little undercover income that kept things precariously afloat. It had been the saving of him—and if all went well it would go on, and on. If all went well . . .

His mind unaccountably turned to the boy who had died in the snow of Hungeren, the boy he had met so briefly. There were rumours going round, talk—but then there was always talk, and half of it contradicted the other half, or was the purest nonsense. There was no reason to believe any one thing people were saying rather than another. No reason to fear the end of his little bonus. And he had always found the police very amenable.

Idling along Storgate in a day full of frustrations and unproductive leads, Inspector Fagermo happened to see, by the open space in front of the Catherdral, two

140

of the people on the fringes of the case whom he had not yet spoken to. On the pavement were planted the two local Mormons, with a hortatory placard, a hail-fellow manner and a promise of salvation available through the combination of Jesus Christ and Joseph Smith. They seemed to have plenty of well-wishers and casual acquaintances, but not many takers. On one of them the Arctic spring seemed to have laid an icy finger: the fair-haired, open-faced one had his tie riotously askew, his jacket and overcoat open, and he was getting as near to chatting up the girls as a street-corner evangelist could reasonably be expected to go. Fagermo stopped by them.

'I've been meaning to look you up,' he said. 'I suppose you can guess what I want to talk about.'

'We told the police we'd be here,' said the heavy one, aggrieved. 'It's our usual time and place.' His Norwegian was very grammatical and highly accented. As old Bostilsrud had said, one never had much doubt with an American.

'Not that,' said Fagermo. 'It's about this murder.' The two faces at once looked mystified and concerned.

'We haven't heard about any murder,' said the fair one. 'Why should we have expected that you'd want to talk to us about a murder?'

'We don't read the papers much,' said the other one. 'We can, but we can't really afford to.'

'I thought it was the main topic of conversation among the foreign community, that's all,' said Fagermo.

'We're more religious,' said the heavy, obstinate one, obscurely.

141

'Anyway, it's about a boy you met, way back before Christmas, in the Cardinal's Hat. I don't know if you remember?'

'The Cardinal's Hat? Were we there?'

'So all the available testimony agrees. I'm sorry if you're not supposed to be.'

'Oh, it's not that so much. But we can't afford eating out or anything, and there's not much we can drink, so I can't quite see why we were there.' The fair boy thought for a bit. 'Wait a minute! I remember now: we did go in one time, just before Christmas.' He turned to his fellow. 'After Steinar, you remember.' He explained to Fagermo: 'It's a boy we've been talking to a lot. He was really getting the message, but he sort of relapses now and then. We've been trying to be good influences, and if we hear of him like going off the rails, we try and get hold of him and talk him out of it, see what I mean?'

Fagermo nodded. It figured: drink and religion were the great weaknesses of a certain type of Norwegian, and some veered enthusiastically from one to the other. He said: 'You went and talked to the foreigners' table there, if you remember.'

'That's right, we did. I suppose we must have known somebody sitting there.'

'Can you recall who?'

The two Mormons thought for a bit. 'There was that man who's an outfitter—has a shop along here somewhere,' said the heavy one. 'He was interested in our suits, said we always looked so smart.'

'We had to tell him they were issued from headquarters,' said the fair one. 'No sale. Then there was an American boy—often see him around—fairly quiet

142

type. Student. And the girl from the USIO: we keep in well with them. They're a lot of help sometimes.'

'Anyone else?'

'There *were* others. I can't recall exactly—'

Fagermo prompted him. 'There was a fair-haired boy, a stranger. You wouldn't have seen him before.'

The two of them thought. 'That's right. Didn't say much. Looked—you know—sort of contemptuous. There's some like that: they look at us like we were some kinda freaks. Yeah, I remember him.' It was the fair-haired one speaking, and Fagermo felt fairly confident he really did remember.

'You didn't talk to him?'

'No, sir. We don't push in where we're not wanted, whatever some people may say. And we were just in looking for Steinar. But I remember seeing that boy again—'

'The boy in the Cardinal's Hat? Where?'

The fair Mormon thought. 'I know I did . . . Not long afterwards, too.'

'It would have been the next day, or the one after.'

'Was it him who got his number?'

'Yes—we found him in the snow above Hungeren.'

The Mormon thought. 'I can't get it. Give me a bit of time, though, and it should come. I'll get on to you as soon as it does. I usually do remember—'

'If you do,' said Fagermo, 'you'll be one of the few to admit remembering anything definite.'

'Part of the training,' said the fair boy, grinning wide and tugging at his crazily askew tie. 'Healthy mind in a healthy body, you know.' He sounded infinitely cynical.

Back in his office Fagermo sat at his desk and

looked over the fjord, glimmering blue and gold like a vulgar evening gown. Things were beginning, just beginning, to make some sort of pattern in his mind. Always he had believed that one of the keys to the case lay in the character of the boy himself. What sort of person was Martin Forsyth? There was still a lot of work to be done there, but he thought the blank outline, symbolized by that anonymous frozen corpse, was beginning to be filled in. But then there was that other vital question: what had Martin Forsyth *been*, what had he *done*? Here there were some pieces in place—pieces from Ålesund, from Trondheim, even from Mersea—but also great gaping blank spaces.

He turned back to his desk and began formulating his second set of questions for Interpol. Precious little he'd got from the first lot: no trace of a criminal record anywhere, not even of any minor involvement in questionable activities, or immigration troubles. But *something* of the boy's past must be recoverable, must be relevant. In fact, he felt sure that something would be crucial, that this was not a murder that could be explained by some sudden burst of passion that sprang up during his three days in Tromsø. He sighed. It was just his luck that Iran was currently in a state of turmoil—a jungle of conflicting forces so complex that none of the great powers seemed to know who to kowtow to. And yet, it was very possible that there some part of the solution might be lying. Aberfan, Mrs Forsyth had said, vaguely. Aberfan, Abadan . . .

He would have to trust to time and returning normality. Meanwhile the only thing to do was to formulate a series of clear, concise, to-the-point questions.

He drew his pad towards him and wrote and thought for half an hour, concentratedly.

When he had finished he picked up his phone and got through to Bjørn Korvald.

'Bjørn? Fagermo here. Do you remember you offered to take me along one night to the Cardinal's Hat? Nothing like being introduced by a friend if you want to break down barriers, is there? Well, what say we make it tonight?'

CHAPTER 13

THE CARDINAL'S HAT

At eight o'clock that evening the Cardinal's Hat was comfortably full, with the usual mixture of students and shop assistants, stray bachelors and stray spinsters, drunken sailors and drunken lecturers. The air was thick with the fumes of beer and frying steak and the smoke of self-rolled cigarettes, but luckily for Fagermo this was not one of the evenings with live jazz. Then you had to bellow your lightest inanities, and take your companion's reply on trust. So up and down the narrow L-shaped room conversation was rife, insults passed from table to table, girls passed from hand to hand, and lonely men on shore leave lurched around in search of confidants for their boozy, lying tales. It was not a smart place: jeans predominated, and heavy jerseys like dead, matted jungle undergrowth. The smart people went to the clubs and the hotel bars, where their sense of importance burgeoned in proportion to the grossness of the overcharging. The clientele of the Cardinal's Hat went there because it was cheap and good; they ranged only from the middling well-off down to the middling hard-up.

Bjørn Korvald and Fagermo collected their litres of beer at the bar counter and pushed their way through the dark-panelled room round to the foreigners' table. For a moment they were not noticed, and Fagermo, gently stopping Bjørn's progress with his hand, had a chance to observe the table and decide that he seemed to have struck it lucky. Crouched over their beers and red wines and Cokes, and deep in a variety of conversations or solitary musings were seven or eight people, and among them were at least two people he was happy to have a chance to speak to away from the inquisitorial atmosphere of the police station. There in the centre, chairman-like, was Helge Ottesen, plump, condescendingly matey, prosperous; and not far away was a young man—flushed, verbose, indignant—whom Fagermo strongly suspected to be the lecturer in French who had been here on the night of Martin Forsyth's visit. For the rest there was a Hong Kong Chinese boy whom he recognized as working at one of the local restaurants, an Algerian student-cum-street-vendor, Dougal Mackenzie, who had found the body, and Steve Cooling, draped enervatedly over a half-bottle of red wine, some of which had streaked a vivid flash across his grubby tee-shirt.

Not a bad haul. But now Bjørn Korvald made a move forward, and the table registered their presence. A sudden hush fell, silencing even the lecturer in French who had been in full self-justifying spate about something or other. The hush was uneasy rather than respectful. Feeling as welcome as the returned Magwitch, they drew back chairs and sat themselves down at the table.

It was Helge Ottesen who broke the silence and did the honours of this informal branch of the Foreigners' Club. With a gesture both nervous and expansive—the

147

behaviour of the fledgling politician in a tight spot—
he half rose, shook hands with Fagermo with an unconvincing smile on his face, and gesturing to left and
right made embryonic introductions around the table.

'Mr . . . er . . . Cooling you know, don't you?
Yes? This is . . . Dr?—no—Herr Botner who teaches
. . . er . . . French at the university, and Dr Mackenzie . . . oh, you've met . . . and, er, Monsieur . . .
and . . . er . . .'

These last introductions were to the Algerian and
the Chinese sitting at the end of the table, quiet and
self-contained, regarding the scene with a genial fasci-
nation that showed they knew exactly who Fagermo
was and why his appearance was received roughly
like that of the spectre at the feast. Ottesen fussed further to cover up the coldness of the welcome.

'It's a pity there are no ladies here tonight. Gives
you the wrong impression. My wife is at a Church ladies meeting, bazaars and things, you know. And
there's usually someone or other here: Miss Bryson
who I think you interv—er, met, didn't you? And we
have the odd librarian and nurse who often drop in.
Really we are not such a—what's the phrase?—such a
male-dominated group as we might seem tonight.'

The tawdry cliché seemed to trigger something in
the French lecturer, who was clearly on the way to
being very nicely drunk indeed.

'Male dominated? Male dominated? Fat chance
these days. *Fat* chance. Have I told you—?'

'Yes,' said Steve Cooling, with that lazy American
tolerance-with-limits. 'Over and over. Put a stopper in
it, can't you?' He turned to Fagermo. 'He's just been

refused a grant for leave, and he's convinced it's because he's a man.'

Botner looked about to explode, and then just as suddenly subsided into his glass. Fagermo took the chance to study him. He was tall, well-fleshed and good-looking in a rather academic, rimless-spectacled way. The type to wear a suit to work, though at the moment his bachelor smartness was looking a little crumpled. He guessed he was the type who might as a rule be reserved, distantly charming, congenitally buttoned-up, but who occasionally broke out. Tonight seemed to be one of the occasions when he broke out.

'Well, of course, we all know who you are,' said Helge Ottesen, unable to conceal that nervous apprehension beneath a gummy smile, but making heroic efforts. 'Is it allowable to ask whether you are on duty now, or is this a visit of pleasure?'

'Oh, pleasure, pleasure,' beamed Fagermo, raising his glass merrily to all and sundry, the ironic glint in his eye telling them that if they believed that, they'd believe anything. 'We policemen have to have time off, you know, when we're not terrorizing the poor motorist, or doing violence to the delinquents by our mere presence on Storgate on Saturday nights. We're human, you know: we like to go out and have a drink, just like anybody else.'

'And is it permitted to ask how the case is going?' asked the slightly Scottish voice of Dougal Mackenzie, the irony in his eye answering that in Fagermo's, and showing that he for one wasn't taken in by Fagermo's night off.

'Oh yes, quite permitted. But I'm not sure I can tell you a great deal at the moment. It's progressing—

progressing in the way cases do. I'm learning more and more, stacking up a little heap of pieces of information. Eventually I'll have to look at them all, discard quite a number of them, and then try to fit the rest together to make up a picture. It's a long process, and very intricate.'

'What you're saying is, the case has wide repercussions, is that it?' asked Steve Cooling.

'If you mean: was it something more than his being slugged by a drunken teenager in a Saturday night brawl, then I'd say *yes*. It's been clear from the beginning that there is more to it than that. Just how much more I can't really decide at this stage.'

'And yet he seemed such a very ordinary young man,' said Helge Ottesen, in an almost pleading voice. 'One really wonders if the sort of thing people are saying—'

'Saying?'

Ottesen was confused and declined to come out into the open. 'Oh, you know, just gossip, gossip.'

'Are they talking about spying? Or oil, perhaps?' Fagermo asked the question casually, but when he put forward the second suggestion he saw Helge Ottesen blink so violently that it almost amounted to a flinch. He could have sworn too that somewhere on the table—where?—there was a flicker of movement from someone else too.

Bjørn Korvald said: 'Whenever anything odd happens in this town people always have explanations like that: Russian activity, American activity, one of the multi-nationals, one of the big oil companies—the more fantastic it is, the more important it makes people up here feel.'

'Absolutely, absolutely,' said Helge Ottesen, with such obvious eagerness that Fagermo marvelled at a politician being so transparent. He raised his eyebrows.

'And yet spying *isn't* unknown around here, is it?' he said. 'All very tin-pot and amateur, no doubt, with one side knowing exactly what the other is up to, and Norway winking at the antics of both because we're a little country and don't want to offend our big friends and neighbours. But it *does* go on, and it could suddenly get serious—like the U2 incident. Then again, we know from Stavanger what sort of effects an oil bonanza would have. It's perfectly obvious that some very big interests do get involved, and some decidedly murky happenings take place. One sometimes finds the fantastic explanation is the only one that makes complete sense.'

There was an uneasy silence. 'So what do you think?' drawled Steve Cooling. 'Was he some kind of small-time spy doing dirty work for one of the oil companies, or what?'

'Oh,' said Fagermo, holding up his hand in protest, 'now we're getting too near the bone. I'm just offering a few conjectures, and I'm not going to tell you what I might or might not *think*. What I've got to do is reconstruct what this boy's life has been like these last few years, since he left school. Reconstruct what *he* was like, come to that. One or other of you that I haven't talked to yet might help me with that. You saw him. What sort of impression did he make on you?' He looked around at the politely hostile faces around the table.

'Cold little sod,' said Botner, looking up from his near-empty glass. He had been drinking steadily and morosely. 'You take . . . you take my word for it—cold little sod.'

Helge Ottesen looked pityingly at Botner and raised a significant eyebrow in Fagermo's direction: 'He was a perfectly well-spoken young chap,' he said. 'Not a great talker, but I'm not sure I like that in young people. All too much of it among the students, I'm sure you'd agree. No, I'd say he was a very responsible young chap, as far as I spoke to him.'

'How far was that? Did you have much conversation?'

'Let me see: not a great deal. But Gladys—that's my wife—Gladys and I tried to make him welcome, since he was a visitor. Told him about the town, what there was going on, what there was to do: the Museum, the churches and so on.'

'You thought he was here for tourism?'

Ottesen blinked. 'Well, not exactly. Not at that time of year. But it was just a sort of introduction to the place.'

'And you didn't talk about anything more personal? Such as his work, for instance?'

Helge Ottesen thought very carefully, with an appearance of trying to remember. 'Let me see. He said he'd worked on boats, which surprised me rather, because he wasn't what I'd call the type. How can I put it, not to seem snobbish? He wasn't at all *rough*.'

Botner threw back his head and roared a drunken laugh. 'Splendidly democratic! Why don't you say he wasn't an obvious yob or an obvious lout and have done with it?'

'Now you're putting words into my mouth. All I meant was that he was rather a—'

'A smooth customer?' suggested Steve Cooling.

'Was he wearing a ring when he came in?' put in Fagermo quickly.

'A ring?' said Ottesen, startled. 'I really couldn't say. Does anyone remember?' He looked round the table. All faces were studiously blank. But this time there *had* been a reaction, a flicker, Fagermo was sure of it.

He said: 'Well, never mind. Just a detail. Are you all agreed then, he was a smooth customer?'

'Well certainly he was nobody's fool,' said Ottesen. 'That's really what I meant. You wouldn't easily put one over him. And though he'd knocked around the world he really seemed to have got something out of it.'

'Ah!' said Fagermo. 'He talked about his travels?'

Ottesen was on his guard at once. 'Er . . . he talked, yes.'

'Where exactly did you gather he'd been?'

'Well, let me see, I'm not sure I remember that he specified . . .'

'If you talked about travel, *some*where must have been specified,' pressured Fagermo.

'Wasn't there some talk about Greece?' suggested Steve Cooling.

'Yes,' said Ottesen quickly. 'I think you're right. Gladys and I went there last year, you know, so I think we talked a bit with him about Rhodes.'

'North Africa? The Gulf States? Iran?' hazarded Fagermo.

'Not that I remember,' said Ottesen uneasily. 'Gladys and I have never been there.'

153

'No package tours to watch the adulterers being stoned? . . . Sorry, just my sense of humour. Well, this has all been very helpful. All the more so since we seem to have two very distinct impressions of young Mr Forsyth. On the one hand, he was respectable, well-spoken, responsible. On the other, he was—I hope I'm not overstating it—cold, calculating, ruthless.'

'The two sides don't entirely rule each other out,' put in Bjørn Korvald.

'By no means. I realize that. And I've met both views before tonight. Two of his girl-friends, for example, would seem to have lived with two entirely different men. But I'd like to hear more about the second view,' said Fagermo, turning in the direction of Botner. 'Because that's more the type that gets murdered, isn't it?'

Botner was clearly not quite with them, but sitting back on his bench gazing vacantly at the ceiling with a petulant expression on his face.

'Don't mind him,' said Dougal Mackenzie. 'He's drinking to forget.'

'I've got a grievance,' said Botner distinctly. 'I've got a bloody grievance. Did I tell you? I was—'

'Yes, you told us,' said Mackenzie.

'Well, I haven't told *him*. I was turned down for leave because I was a man. Of the male sex. Masculine in gender.'

'Oh, don't talk crap,' pleaded Steve Cooling.

'Let him have his say,' said Fagermo. 'Then we can talk about something else.'

This seemed to sting Botner. 'Oh, uppity, aren't we? Well, I tell you it's true. There's not a penny piece for anyone these days unless they're studying *women's* literature, or *women*'s history, or women's bloody grammar for all I know. If you're not studying role stereotypes for women in the negro novel or some goddam thing like that, you haven't got a *hope*. It's discrimination, that's what it is! We've become the bloody underdogs!'

'Well, now you've had your say,' said Steve Cooling, 'and it's a pity you couldn't do it a bit softer because there's such a thing as lynch law where that subject is concerned, perhaps you could tell the gentleman what he wants to know?'

'What gentleman?' asked Botner, pulling himself to an upright position and looking round the table.

'I was wondering,' said Fagermo, 'now you've told us your grievance, which was very interesting, if you could say why you thought Martin Forsyth was—what was your expression?—such a cold little sod.'

'Because I remember watching him.' Now he had got away from his sorrows he was speaking more naturally. 'He was just here by chance, you know, just dropped in—or so he said—but there were certain things he did instinctively. Like right from the moment he sat down at this table he was alert to find out who was the most important person at the table. He just did it instinctively.' He looked round triumphantly at the rest of the table to see if they were impressed by his perceptiveness, but he met studious blankness. 'Well, he decided that self-important twit Nicolaisen was the most important—which is a bit of a joke, and shows he wasn't as bright as you lot have been trying to make out. Anyway, he tried talking to him first, but he didn't get anywhere, because our Halvard doesn't like the young, and more especially young men, for reasons we all know and needn't go into, so he saw he wasn't getting through and he switched round and let old Ottesen prose on at him—opps, sorry! Forgot you were here!'

'Oh now, I say—' said Helge Ottesen, but whether in protest at being allotted only secondary importance or at this interpretation of Martin Forsyth's behaviour was not quite clear.

'And then, he was good at getting beer bought for him. I don't think he bought one after his first. Both that poor little Bryson girl, who has to count every penny, and that streak of nothing Cooling—there I go again!—bought him drinks just before they left: he knew he wouldn't have to buy them one in return.'

'I've known other people at this table do the same,' said Mackenzie, with Scottish wisdom.

'And then he let that girl pour out her boring little life story to him, just because he knew she was an easy lay. I was sitting opposite him and I could see he wasn't listening to a single word, just thinking about his own concerns.'

'Hell—if you go by that we must all be cold little sods, because we've all done the same,' said Steve Cooling.

'Wait, wait. He let her give him her address before she left, and he made some sort of a date with her, but after she'd gone he looked at me and said: "In case nothing better turns up." Just like that. Do you see? He was a right bastard. He was ashamed, not because he'd led her on, but because she's so boring and ordinary. He wanted me to know he was used to a better class of girl than that. For Christ sake get me a drink, someone. I've talked myself dry as a bone.'

Bjørn Korvald obligingly got up, collected glasses and set off for the bar. Satisfied, Botner continued: 'So I doubt if he ever turned up in *her* bed.'

'He couldn't,' said Fagermo. 'He was dead.'

'Well, he wouldn't have anyway,' said Botner, 'because he went on to something better.'

'Oh? How do you know?'

'I saw him! The next night, with a woman.'

'Oh, you did, did you? A blonde, I presume, is that right?'

'Oh, you know.' Botner looked deflated. 'I thought I was telling you something new. I might have known there were plenty of others who saw them.'

'Was this on Biskopsvei, above the kiosk there?'

'Oh no, no.' Botner seemed to be trying to concentrate. 'Not there. If I'd seen them there I'd have been in my car. And I wasn't in my car. Was I?' He looked around appealingly.

'Let's take it as read that he wasn't in his car,' said Dougal Mackenzie.

'Well, then, if I wasn't in my car, where would I be?'

'Going to see Marit?' suggested Steve Cooling.

'Got it! Got it! I was going to see Marit. She's one of the girls around the place, you know. I go there sometimes. So does Steve. Sometimes we meet in the street and toss up. That's it. I was on foot, somewhere between my flat and Marit's house. There you are. Now you know.'

'If you could tell me where your flat is, and Marit's house.'

'Oh yes—on the edges of Håpet. That's where we both live. A bit of a university slum. And this boy— what was his name?—Forsyth, and this girl, this

157

woman rather, blonde, thirtyish, thirty-five maybe, they were walking along, he with his arm around her, casual, and she talking very high and fast. That's it. And I know where it was. I've got it. It was the corner of Elgveien. They were turning in. He saw me over his shoulder—saw me and grinned. That's how I know. That's how I know he was a cool, slimy bastard.'

'Elgveien,' said Helge Ottesen. 'Elgveien.' He looked up at Bjørn Korvald returning with two glasses of beer. 'Isn't that where you . . . where you used to live, Bjørn?'

Half-way through the question he had faltered, and an air of profound embarrassment came over him.

CHAPTER 14

WIFE OF A FRIEND

The goodbyes as Fagermo and Bjørn Korvald left the Cardinal's Hat were genial but edged with unease, like a schoolboy's to his teachers on the last day, uncertain of what relationship each might have with the other in the future. Fagermo was urged to come back often, but like the schoolboy he felt he would not. A policeman does not mingle casually like other men: how many of the normal topics of conversation in the Cardinal's Hat would be discussed with equal freedom with a policeman there? He and Bjørn fought their way through the fug to the cold, clear darkness outside, and stood together uncertainly on the icy pavement.

'I think we'd better talk,' said Fagermo abruptly. 'Where shall we go? My office?'

Bjørn nodded unhappily, and they trudged the two minutes' walk past the SAS Hotel and round to the station. As soon as he swung open the door to his office Fagermo realized his mistake. The room was dominated by his desk, and the only natural place for him to sit was behind it. It was no place for a heart-to-heart with a friend about the friend's wife. With a sigh he accepted the inevitable, took off his coat, and sat himself on the swivel chair.

'I'm sorry about this,' he said to Korvald. 'Not exactly cosy, but the only people I usually entertain here are suspects or witnesses. Still, at least we're not likely to be interrupted. Pull up a chair and make yourself comfortable.'

Bjørn Korvald pulled up a chair, but could hardly make himself comfortable: seated opposite that intimidating desk he seemed immediately to fit into that slot marked 'suspect'—or, worse, that slot marked 'informer'. It seemed to affect him adversely. He sat there grimly, waiting for Fagermo to begin.

'Well, let's get it over with,' said Fagermo. 'You realize as well as I do what everyone there tonight was thinking.' Bjørn nodded. 'It's a small road, Elgveien, isn't it? How many houses would you say were in it altogether?'

Bjørn thought: 'Not more than seven, I suppose. And most of them single-family houses.'

'Yes. And this Botner saw a blonde woman going into it with Martin Forsyth, the night before the murder, in all probability. I'm putting it bluntly, you see. Is there anyone else in the street the description might fit?'

Bjørn sat with his head in his hands. 'Most of the families are older than us. I practically ruined myself building there. There are two couples in their sixties. Three I suppose in their fifties. One of them has a teenage daughter . . .'

'It didn't sound like a teenager.'

'No, it didn't. I suppose my—my *wife* is the obvious one.'

'That's what I was thinking. Do you mind if we talk about her a bit?'

Bjørn Korvald looked as if he minded a lot. Suddenly he had lost all that air of youth regained that Fagermo had noticed in him since he had left his wife. His shoulders sagged, his face-muscles were relaxed like a gassed soldier's. He seemed to want nothing so much as solitude to think. But Fagermo decided he had better talk now, and be done with it.

'I'd better tell you what I know about this blonde. Tonight wasn't the first time I'd heard of her. As far as we know they met some way up Biskopsvei on the night after Forsyth was in the Cardinal's Hat— probably the day before he was murdered, as I say. Whether they'd met before we don't know. Perhaps— but our witness thought, and our witness is a sharp old body I wouldn't like to contradict. She thought, in fact—sorry to have to say this, Bjørn, she thought that one picked up the other.'

Korvald looked up, great thick lines along his forehead, but he flapped a hand dismissively: 'No, no—it's nothing to me. Would to God she had someone. But not *him*.'

'Exactly. Not him, and not him *then*. But we've got to take the facts as we find them, as we always do in my job. Let's take it as a hypothesis, nothing more, that she was walking down Biskopsvei, and stopped him and talked to him on one pretext or other. Now— does that surprise you? She was twenty minutes or so's walk from home.'

Bjørn Korvald straightened. 'Well, not entirely, to tell you the truth. Once or twice people have mentioned that they've seen her, on her own. Don't know why they tell me. Busybodies, I suppose. And one evening, coming home, I thought I caught a glimpse of her—near where I have my flat.'

'Spying on you, do you think?'

'Something of the sort is what I thought. Perhaps wanting to know if there's any other woman. There isn't, by the way.'

'What about the children? What have you got?'

'Two little girls. Five and seven. That's what's been worrying me, of course. But I've no evidence that she's often out at night. They're very good sleepers, and in fact she may well get a baby-sitter in. What occurred to me was . . .'

'Yes?'

'It's just an idea, but I thought she might want to *prove* something—to the neighbours, and so on. She always worried about the neighbours.'

'What sort of thing?'

'That she wasn't lonely, went out a lot, had heaps of friends, that sort of thing.'

'I get you. And it wouldn't be true?'

'No, it wouldn't. It was always just the home with her, and the children of course. And me, I suppose, in a way. So I just thought that, having got a baby-sitter in, she might have to go out. And she'd have nowhere to go.'

'It's pretty pathetic.'

'Don't I know it. I've tried—but anyway, we're not talking about my domestic problems. The point is, I think she'd like to know what I've been doing. Perhaps she's been around more often than I've seen. Or perhaps she's made a habit of picking men up. I'm afraid I'm pretty remote from her now, so I really wouldn't know.'

'How often do you see her?'

'Once a week, when I go for the kids. Not always then. Often they're watching for me, and they run out. And sometimes they come to me by bus.'

'What sort of state would you say she was in? Mental state?'

Bjørn said reluctantly: 'Not too good, I'd say.' He was clearly a battle-ground of conflicting emotions that told him that he *was* responsible and was *not* responsible, *was* involved and was well out of it. He said: 'It's difficult to know what to do. I couldn't go back to her and stay sane, not after I've had my freedom. But there's nothing else would satisfy her. No—not even that would. It just *shouldn't have happened.* She simply can't face up to the fact that it did, it has happened. She has no idea *why.* She's as bewildered now as the day I said I was getting out. The only thing that would really put her little world together would be to wake up and find it was all a dream. So really there's nothing I can do.'

'The question is,' said Fagermo, 'what should I do? I'll have to go and talk to her. How should I approach her? Do you think she'll deny it?'

'I think she may well,' said Bjørn. 'She doesn't have any beautiful abstract passion for truth, certainly. I suppose nobody much does, these days. And you've got to remember that there's no proof it was her.'

'No, no. Still, we've got Botner. If necessary we could have him identify her. I shouldn't think she'd want things to go so far—that is, if she's nothing worse to hide than a night with a stranger. Do you think there's any way of getting her on my side—palling up with her? It would make it easier.'

Bjørn thought. 'I'll tell you how I see her. I think she has always lived in a fairy-tale world in which she is the perfect woman, the perfect wife, the perfect mother. Her mother coached her in what she had to do and be when she married, and she fulfilled her instructions to the letter, and lived in a kind of dream in which she was sanctified by virtue of her clean windows and aired sheets. Do you get me? She's self-righteous without being religious. If you're going to say anything that smashes that image she has of herself, I think she's going to deny it, I'm afraid, however you approach her.'

'So—no chink in the armour?'

'If there is one, I never found it.'

'Try around eleven-thirty,' Bjørn Korvald had said to Fagermo before he left. 'Åse should be at school, and with a bit of luck Karen will be playing with the neighbours' little boy.'

So at eleven-thirty, with the sun shining in a postcard blue sky and the temperature edging over zero, Fagermo trudged up the snow-lined path to the house Bjørn and Sidsel Korvald had built for themselves in their less than blissful married years. It was a moderate-sized wooden house, with a built-in garage and large plate-glass windows, unnaturally clean, on the first floor. He rang the bell—electronic, two notes with an interval—and looked at the lead-lighted coloured windows around the heavy wooden front door.

Sidsel Korvald was prompt in answering, opening the door with a automatic smile switched on simultaneously with the turning of the doorknob: 'Yes?'

She was doing a very good performance of an ordinary Norwegian housewife on an ordinary day of the week, going about her ordinary business. That it *was* a performance Fagermo realized by that sixth policeman's sense, which is a combination of sad experience and common-sense psychology. There was strain in the lines of the forehead, a haunted, inward-looking anxiety in the eyes. But the mouth put up a show of confidence and welcome, and she was boringly neat as a pin.

'Fru Korvald? I wonder if I could talk to you for a few minutes? My name is Fagermo—I'm from the police.'

She showed no sign of stepping aside to let him in, and the smile was extinguished. 'My husband doesn't live here at the moment,' she said.

'It was you I wanted to speak to,' said Fagermo. Then, lowering his voice considerably, a thing he wouldn't have done for Professor Nicolaisen, he said: 'It's a matter of some importance. I think it would be better if we could go inside.'

She looked at him with a wild glint of fear, the mouth now set in a resentful straight line. But finally she stood aside, and Fagermo went determinedly through the hall and upstairs to the living-room. She followed him with every appearance of feeling deeply injured by his call. As if to make something or other plain to him she looked at his shoes and did not ask him to sit down. He sat down.

'I'm sorry to barge in like this, Fru Korvald,' he

said, 'but believe me, it's going to be easier if we try to talk things over in a friendly way.'

She pursed her lips together, said nothing, but finally sat down on the sofa, her knees close together, her hands clasped in her lap. As he was trying to think up a way of approaching her, she suddenly blurted out, as if clutching at a straw that had already proved its fragility: 'If it's anything to do with money, I think you ought to see my husband. He sees to all the bills and things.'

'It's nothing to do with money,' said Fagermo gently. 'It concerns a boy—a young man—you may have read about him. He was found dead, murdered, over in Hungeren.'

'Oh yes?'

Her clamlike stance was more revealing than a more gushing response would have been. Of course she must have read about the murder. Fagermo said: 'No doubt you will have read about it in *Nordlys*.'

'I may have,' she said, as though the words were being prised out of her. 'I don't have much time . . .'

'Did it occur to you when you read about it, that you might have known the young man?'

'Certainly not!' The words shot out bitterly, shocked but without surprise. 'Why should I have known him? He was a foreigner, wasn't he?'

'That's right. English.'

'Well, then.' She subsided into silence, as if she had proved a point.

'And yet, I think you did know him. I think you met him one night just before Christmas, up on Biskops-vei. Or perhaps you had met him before?'

'No!'

166

'No, you hadn't met him before?'

'No—I don't know what you're talking about! Biskopsvei is miles from here. What would I be doing there at night?'

'That I don't know. I don't suppose it's of any importance. What is important is that you met this boy—Martin Forsyth his name was, by the way—up in Biskopsvei, just above the kiosk.'

'I deny it. You're talking nonsense.'

'I see. There could, of course, have been some mistake. But we have several witnesses. I'm afraid I shall have to arrange an identity parade . . .'

Sidsel Korvald's mouth was working convulsively. 'I don't understand what you're saying. Why should I go through an identity parade? What are you accusing me of?'

'Nothing. Nothing whatsoever.'

'Then this is just—persecution!'

'Fru Korvald, the only reason I have to get you to confirm that you met Martin Forsyth that night is because I have to trace *all* his movements in the two days before he was murdered. Can you see that? It would have been much easier for you if you had come forward yourself when the case first came into the papers. Now I can see that you find it hard, and embarrassing. I'm sorry about that. But as far as we can gather he was seen alive after you met him. We have no suspicions of you. You need have no hesitations about speaking. Only please tell the truth—and tell *all* the truth.'

He leaned back in his chair. What he had said was not perhaps as impeccably truthful as he had enjoined her to be, but he had the satisfaction of watching it sink into the pretty, empty, self-absorbed face of the woman opposite. He let the ball settle down in her side of the court, and waited long minutes for her to say something.

'What do you want to know, then?' The words came very low, reluctant.

'How did you come to meet Martin Forsyth?'

'I . . . I met him on Biskopsvei, as you said, one night. I, well, I asked him the time.'

'You were doing—what?'

'Walking. Just walking.' She saw him watching her, waiting for more, and she burst out: 'I've had a lot of troubles. You don't know. I've been shamefully treated. I need to walk sometimes. To think.' A nerve in her cheek began to twitch uncontrollably, making her left eye blink grotesquely.

'Yes, I had heard that,' said Fagermo.

She cast a suspicious look, as if to enquire who he had been talking to, but getting no response, her grievance took hold of her again, and she spat out: 'Can you understand how—how a man who has a lovely home, and lovely children, and everything made easy for him, just as he likes it, can just get up and go off? Not go off with anyone, but just go off? Off to some nasty little room, and live on his own? Can you explain it?'

The voice was like a wailing saxophone, full of humiliation and despair. Fagermo felt no compulsion to answer honestly, and he said gently: 'It must be difficult to understand.'

'I can explain it. He's mad. That's the answer. There must be madness in his family somewhere. He's taken leave of his senses.'

She subsided a little. This was clearly an answer her walking had evolved, the only possible solution to her personal conundrum.

'So you were just walking, and thinking. That's very understandable. But you talked to Forsyth for a little while, didn't you? What about?'

'I suppose about—about his being a foreigner, and what he was doing in Tromsø at that time of year. Things like that.'

'And then you asked him back here?'

For a moment all rage and shame seemed to have left her, and she answered dully: 'Yes,' adding, as if not expecting to be believed: 'For coffee.' Then, with some of the old defiance she said: 'You don't know what it's like, only having children to talk to all day long. I get *sick* for a grown-up voice.'

'I can imagine,' said Fagermo. He could, too. 'What did you talk about? Yourself? Him?'

'Oh, we talked about him. A man doesn't want to be burdened with a woman's problems, does he? I—I asked him to tell me about himself.'

It sounded like a whore's ploy, but Fagermo blessed her for it. 'That's what I was hoping. What did he tell you?'

'Well, we came home and in fact we—we had a drink. I had some in, for Christmas. I have a lot of friends who might call.' No friends, no calls, thought Fagermo. 'So we walked back, and it was nice to have someone to—to lean on, and we sat down and I got drinks, and he told me about his travels. It was fascinating. Such interesting things, wonderful places.'

'What sort of things, places?'

She drew her hand over her forehead distractedly.

The strain was telling. She had to think, hard. She hadn't listened, thought Fagermo; she hadn't been interested. 'I remember a lot about Greece,' she said finally. 'About a shipping millionaire's yacht. He'd been a crew member. Not one of the millionaires you read about . . . And then there were a lot of Arab places, I don't remember their names, but it was . . . fascinating. And then Iran. I remember that because it was in the news, and of course I'd seen pictures of the Shah and his wife. Isn't it awful about them? Yes, I remember he talked about Iran.'

'What sort of things did he tell you about? Was it mostly about his work?'

'Yes, I think so. He had worked there, definitely. Something to do with oil, I think. I remember the names you see in garages. Yes—I'm sure he had worked a lot with oil.'

'Can you be more specific?'

The hand went over her forehead again. 'No. I mean I didn't really understand . . . And of course we talked about other things as well—'

'I suppose things got more—personal, did they?' Fagermo hated doing it, but he had to know the sort of terms the two ended on.

She flushed up, and the twitch on the side of her face, which had stopped working and distorting her china good looks, began again with redoubled intensity. 'I know what you mean. I know what you're implying. Well, why not? I'm not ashamed.'

'I'm not trying to suggest that you should be.'

'What is a woman to do when her husband—goes off his head? Just settle down calmly and forget all about—that sort of thing? Nobody does these days!'

170

'I know,' said Fagermo. 'Please put it out of your head that I'm trying to put you on trial. It's not even something I'm particularly interested in.'

Her face was crimson now, and her eyes were full. 'So long as it's understood that I'm not ashamed.'

'Absolutely. But before things got more . . . down to earth, did he tell you anything about his personal life?'

'Not much. He was quite reserved, in a way, at that stage. He said he'd been living with a girl in Trond-heim.'

'That's true. Did he say anything about his life before that?'

'No—we didn't go that far back. As a matter of fact, that wasn't what he wanted to talk about. Not about his personal life.'

'Oh?'

'Well, you don't, do you? Not when you're with an-other woman.'

Fagermo took her point. 'But you must have got some impression, through all this talk, of what sort of a boy—man—he was. What he was like.'

She pondered, the flush hardly diminished, and her face seemed to be suppressing memories of some bit-terness. She said in a low voice: 'Very self-contained. Very confident. Not very . . . giving.' Then suddenly she looked at him straight, her eyes full of tears, and almost cried out: 'You know the sort of person! Who doesn't give a damn about anyone but themselves! I've had enough of people like that!'

Fagermo looked unhappily at his knees, she seemed so utterly to fit the category she described. 'You think that's the sort of person he was, do you?'

She almost wailed: 'I know it! I know it! All I wanted was a little tenderness!'

'And you didn't get it?'

'Get it? He wasn't capable of it! It wasn't in him! He just used me!' Now she was working herself up with remembered rage, the nerve in her face going double time at the thought of her humiliation. 'Do you know what I was to him? I was a pick-up. An easy lay. He did what he wanted, and that was an end to it. The only difference was he didn't have to pay, and that was the sort of thing he thought about, believe me. He had saved money. There wasn't an *ounce* of feeling in it. He didn't know I was a person. I'll tell you what he was: he was a machine! A beautifully maintained machine!'

'Is that why you . . . got rid of him? That *is* what happened, isn't it?'

She nodded. 'Yes. I got rid of him. I don't know if I can make you understand. After all, I know how men think. I expect you're saying "Well, she picked him up, didn't she? That's what she wanted. What's she complaining about?" Oh, you can't tell me anything about men!' But suddenly she seemed to forget her grievance and speak honestly. 'He made me feel *dirty*. Filthy. It was the way he talked . . .'

'Talked?'

'All the time in here. And then in bed, after . . . The way he talked. It sort of built up. He was so . . . full of himself. How smart he was. How he was up to everybody's tricks, and knew tricks worth two of theirs. Silly jargon like that. Then he kept talking about the ways he had of "making a quick buck". He had some other expression, what was it? "An easy kill".' She stopped in her tracks. 'Funny when you think about it, isn't it? But what I hated . . . what was so insulting that I couldn't stand it any longer was *why* he spoke to me like that—'

'Why? What do you mean?'

'Well, I don't suppose he talked like that to everyone. In fact, early on he was quite—as I said—quite self-contained. But then he decided I was nobody. Something he'd picked up off the streets. He found out who my parents were—nobody important—he knew I had no connections any longer with my husband. So I didn't matter, I couldn't harm him. After we—in bed, it got worse. It was like I was his whore, and he paid me to listen to him talking, as well . . . He just *swelled* with his own cleverness. He was going places. The world was still open to a smart operator, it was still possible to "do an Onassis" as he called it— get rich quick. He knew a thing or two that nobody else knew. He just lay there, talking on and on. About how damned smart he was. About his plans. His big plans. He'd made me feel dirty before. Now I felt like some rotten accomplice.'

'What sort of plans was this he was talking about? Did he go into any details?'

'I didn't listen very much. I was getting—worked up, I suppose. Angry, I mean. Just lying there, feeling ignored. I'd served my purpose, and now he could get back to thinking about himself and his great prospects. His shining future. How he was going to do down this person, double-cross that.'

'Do down? Double-cross? Can't you remember any details? It's very important! Think!'

'Oh, does it matter, does it matter?' She drew her

hand across her wet eyes. She felt nothing about the boy's murder, that was clear. If anything, glad. Seeing Fagermo watching her, she seemed to pull herself together and try to think. 'It was to do with information. Facts. Data. I don't know what you'd call it. I remember he lay there, with his hands behind his head looking so . . . complacent. And he said something like: "So many people want it. Everyone's interested. That's why I went into this business. It's a sure-fire thing. If you play your cards right you can sell the same info over and over again." Those aren't his exact words. Does it make sense?'

'Yes, it could.'

'And he said: "And then, you see, if you channel the info cleverly, that gives you a hold on the middleman. Once you've done shady business with someone, he's yours—if he's respectable and you've nothing to lose. If you play your cards right, you can squeeze him, too." I didn't understand what he meant.'

'I think I do. Anything else?'

'Oh, I expect so. Plenty more. I just lay there, feeling ignored, and it just washed over me. And it was all very vague—he wanted me to admire his cleverness, but he wouldn't give too much away. He just went on and on, and I lay there, listening to him, and getting sicker and sicker—with him.' She stopped and added emphatically: 'With *him,* not with myself.'

'And then what happened? He didn't just go.'

She smiled, a smile of strange self-satisfaction, giving Fagermo the idea that what had happened that night was a clash of two overweening egotisms. 'I threw him out. I listened and listened, and finally I couldn't stand it any more, and I got up and threw his clothes at him, and screamed and screamed: "Get out, get out, get out." '

'And he did?'

'Yes, he did. He just got up and dressed, with me screaming at him, and him looking at me . . . sort of, not understanding . . . supercilious. As if he was saying "Stupid woman".' For a moment she looked uncertain, but then she put a confident front on it: 'Then he slunk from the house.' She smiled complacently. 'I don't think he really understood.'

That, Fagermo thought, was probably the problem with Martin Forsyth. He never really understood.

CHAPTER 15

BLOOD IN THE *VINDFANG*

In the course of the next morning Fagermo began to feel the mist imperceptibly rising. That it did so was not the result of any of the international enquiries he had set in motion. Very little had come out of the series of questions he had sent to Interpol. The situation in Iran was such that Westerners were fleeing the country like migrating birds, so concerned to escape the firing-squad, the whip or the bastinado that they even tactfully refrained from enquiring about duty-free grog at the airport. In such circumstances of chaos and panic, little was to be expected from officials of the major oil companies. Feeling helpless, Fagermo decided it was time to turn his attentions to those companies' head offices in Britain and the States, and made contacts with Scotland Yard and the FBI with this in view.

But the first really valuable piece of jigsaw to turn itself up in the box that morning came in the shape of the fair-haired Mormon who enquired for him in the outer office, and was shuffled by Hyland straight up to Fagermo.

'Good morning,' said Fagermo. 'Where's Tweedle-dee?'

'I've just seen him off at the airport,' said the young man. His going seemed to have made a difference to his companion: he still wore his suit, probably his only gear, but underneath his tie was discarded, and his hair was in a ruffled state and generally far from Madison Avenue. The boy seemed to feel the need to explain his state of liberation. 'He'll be back in Salt Lake City by tomorrow, turning in his suit. Gee, I envy him. I've got six months to do. But his replacement doesn't arrive until tonight.'

'You must feel lost on your own,' said Fagermo. 'Tell me, do you always go around in twos?'

'Well, mostly. It prevents unfortunate happenings. There was a young Mormon chap in Britain recently—'

'Ah yes, I remember,' said Fagermo, who sometimes bought an English Sunday paper when the seamy side of Tromsø life was beginning to seem uninventive. 'I can see that you have to take care. Well, what can I do for you?'

'I've remembered where I saw this chap—the boy who was murdered. Is that any help?'

'Could well be. Depends on how definite you can be.'

'Pretty definite, as it happens. You see, the fact is, we have a pretty set routine: we do certain areas at certain times—I mean the going round and knocking on doors and giving our spiel, you know. We have it all planned out well in advance and written down: on such and such a day we do these streets in Håpet; on such and such one we do those in Kroken, and so on.'

'Just like salesmen.'

'I reckon. So the fact is, if I can remember *where* I saw him, that also tells me *when* I saw him. Right?'

177

'I see. Sounds just what we need.'

'That's what I thought. Now, I'll tell you where I saw him: we were coming down from Nordselvei into Anton Jakobsensvei. It's mostly naval wives around there, and they're often lonely and ask us in just for a chat, especially those that've been to the States. I've had—well, never mind. Anyway, we tend to knock off round about two, because people start cooking their *middags* then. So it was *around* that time—couldn't be more definite than that. Anyway, he was coming along Anton Jakobsensvei from the town end, as if he'd walked over the bridge. I just about recognized him through the gloom, and I was going to stop and talk to him.'

'Why were you going to do that? I thought he hadn't expressed any great interest in your line.'

'Hell, no, but nobody much is interested, except students writing papers on us and things like that. But we like to keep tabs on the English-speakers in town, just for someone to talk to.'

'And did you talk to him?'

'No, we didn't, because he turned off: before we got down to where the road forks he'd turned off down into Isbjørnvei.'

'And kept on going down there?'

'I guess so. We didn't follow him, because we were on our way home. But in any case, you can't really *go* anywhere down that road—only Isbjørnvei and Binnavei just above. Binnavei's full of university people, and so's the first part of Isbjørnvei: they shut the door on us like we were the curse of Dracula. Must have something to hide, I guess. Then along Isbjørnvei there are some more naval people—they're O.K. Then round the loop in the road there are some people employed in the Town Council offices. Real snooty, some of that lot. But anyways, I guess this guy must have had a date with someone or other in those three groups down there.'

'That,' said Fagermo, 'is what I'd guess too. Now—when was this? Can you be absolutely exact?'

'Yes, I can,' said the Mormon boy, taking out his diary for the previous year. 'Every month we enter up the area to be canvassed each day, and we only depart from it if something *very* special or unexpected turns up. In other words, virtually never. Right?'

'Right,' said Fagermo, impressed in spite of himself by the Big Company efficiency of the whole futile operation.

'In my eighteen months here I only remember us changing schedule once—about a year ago, because of Easter: the holiday was longer than we'd calculated. Right? So this is a regular record—' tapping the diary—'of where we were, and when. And it says we did the far end of Anton Jakobsensvei and up to Nordselvei on December twenty-first. So it was coming down from there, some time I'd guess between one-thirty and two-fifteen, that we saw this boy.'

He leaned back in his chair with a self-congratulatory smile on his fair, open face.

'I'm impressed,' said Fagermo. 'Tell me one thing, though. You've told me how you can be sure *when* it was you saw him, but how come you're so sure *where* it was? People don't remember so exactly as a rule.'

For a moment the young man looked embarrassed. 'Well, hell, we're trained in that kind of thing—cultivating the memory—it goes with the job . . .

But, well, if you want to know, something had just happened that made everything stand out in my mind that day. I'd—well, I'd just met a girl—'

'Really? I thought Tweedledee was there to protect you against things of that kind.'

'Yes, well, that's the idea. And he did his best, by Chr—George he did. But sometimes it happens you can—sort of—get a message across without talking. Right?'

Mindful of Fru Nicolaisen, Fagermo began to wonder why the human race had ever taken to speech. 'So I believe.'

'And well, I let him talk to the parents, and let him get all bogged down with his diagrams—we have a lot of diagrams, but Joseph, he wasn't too hot with them—and, well, while all that was going on I sort of—well, I suppose you could say I made eyes at the daughter. Or we made them at each other. And I managed a date before we got out of the door. So you see, I was all keyed up when I saw this boy, and I suppose that's why I remember exactly where.'

'Well, well,' said Fagermo, 'it all sounds practically Shakespearean. I didn't know such things happened these days. I trust the course of true love has run smooth?'

'Pretty much so, but it's getting time alone that's the problem. Joseph was pretty hot on the rules.' He got up. 'So I'll be getting along, O.K.? She's got the day off *gymnas* today. Sick. We've got till eleven-fifteen tonight, when I have to meet the plane. See you around, O.K.?'

'I expect so,' said Fagermo. 'Oh, just one more question: do you ever actually make any converts?'

The boy paused in the doorway and scratched his chin: 'Well, no. Not what you'd call converts. Lots of people are interested, but they don't actually—come over. We're really just sort of showing the flag. What you might call maintaining a presence in the area!'

And he breezed out. So that was it. They were the spiritual equivalent of a NATO base. Fagermo meditated on this idea for some time, then shrugged it from him, regretfully.

Moving house is always a business, and Norwegians like to do things thoroughly. No good Norwegian housewife would want to move into a house that was not, from the beginning, spotlessly clean. Fru Dagny Andersen was a very good Norwegian housewife, and she had made it clear to the removers, her husband, her friends back in Bergen and anyone else who would listen (for she was a thoroughly tedious woman) that she needed three solid days' cleaning in this new house before the family could be moved from Bergen to Tromsø, where her husband was taking up a Professorship in Reindeer Husbandry.

So there she was, with a sleeping-bag and lots of plastic buckets, with a rigidly classified collection of cloths and mops, giving the house a thorough going over from ceiling to basement before the removal men could be permitted to unload their household effects into it. She scrubbed, scoured, washed and polished, her whole body sweating in the spring sunshine, her mind almost blank but for the topics of rival cleaning fluids, and washing powders, and a dreadful generalized feeling of self-righteousness.

'They *said* it was done,' she said with a smug smile

to Fru Vibe, her neighbour, as she passed on her way to the shop, 'but it never is, is it? Not *properly*. I wouldn't have wanted to bring my family into *this*. Not the state this place was in. I like to know a place is really *clean*.'

And Fru Vibe kept her end up by agreeing whole-heartedly, and with lots of housewifely detail about corners and bottom cupboards, though in her heart of hearts she did have a slight sense that cleanliness could be carried too far.

But now Fru Andersen was coming to the end of her tasks. The hall had been done, and the downstairs bedroom and the store cupboards, and now, with the front door open to let in the afternoon sun she was beginning on the *vindfang*, the little square place just inside the front door, designed to keep draughts out and protect the blessed greenhouse quality of the Norwegian home. Even a *vindfang* should be clean, and be *seen* to be clean, she said to herself compla-cently.

But when Fru Vibe came home from the shop an hour or so later she found Fru Andersen still on the floor, still at it, and in far from happy mood.

'They said it had been done,' she said, stopping her scrubbing and poising herself on her haunches. 'But look at that.' She pointed to a brown mark on the skirting-board near the floor. 'It's not mud, I know that. I've been at it for nearly half an hour, and I can't get it out. I think it must be blood.'

Something stirred, uncomfortably, in Fru Vibe. Of course, it couldn't be, it was impossible, and yet . . . It was as well to be sure. Something close to fear seized her stomach. Her solution, in all matters of doubt or complaint, was to dump the topic in the lap of Lindestad, the housing officer of the university. After all, they were the landlords.

'I should give up scrubbing,' said Fru Vibe. 'I'll ring up Lindestad and tell him to have a look.'

As luck would have it, Fagermo was sitting in Lindestad's office in the University Administration building when the call came through. Lindestad, a tough little man with a gnome face, was a rare specimen of omnicompetence, with an elephant's memory and the ability to fix anything that went wrong in his domain— which was what he usually did do, rather than undergo the frustrations of trying to get outside men to do it. But it was his memory that Fagermo was interested in at the moment.

'The girl next door said it would take time to get the information,' he said. 'She had to go through her files, I suppose. She said it would be quicker to talk to you.'

Lindestad grinned with amiable modesty. 'What do you want to know?'

'Well, basically this: who was in the university houses in Isbjørnvei in December of last year—that for a start. I gather there are flats in them as well, and I'd like to know who was in those as well.'

Lindestad thought and drew towards him a piece of paper. He wrote down the numbers of the university houses, and after some thought put down by them a list of names. 'These are the main tenants,' he said, 'of the houses that were occupied. The flats are a bit more difficult.'

He pushed the list towards Fagermo, and it was at

this moment that the phone rang. As Lindestad answered a patient and monotonous yes to the upbraiding voice on the other end of the line, Fagermo studied the list. But when Lindestad said 'Blood?' he looked up with a definite flicker of interest. As Lindestad put the phone down with a promise to come out and see, Fagermo said: 'Blood? Where was that?'

'Isbjørnvei. Are you interested?'

'Too right I'm interested. What number?'

'Let's see. Must be eighteen. New people moving in today.'

Fagermo looked down his list and with a pang of disappointment saw by the number eighteen the one word 'vacant'.

'Was there no one at all there in December?' he asked.

'No one in the main part of the house, anyway,' said Lindestad, getting up. 'These houses are kept for Professors and the like: really it's a sort of ghetto for upper-rank academics. They're often vacant for a fair while, being kept for someone or other. This one has been vacant from last summer right up to now.'

'What about the flat?'

'Let's see . . . I think it's someone in the library . . . Yes, that's right. Don't remember her name—rather a pathetic-looking creature.'

Fagermo shook his head. That hardly sounded promising. 'Let's go and have a look, anyway.'

When they got there they left the car below the road, down by the garages that served the houses, and as they climbed through the snow to Isbjørnvei Fagermo was aware of a face watching them from No. 12. Fru Nicolaisen, no doubt, perhaps hoping for a visit from her policeman lover. Shielding their eyes from the golden glare of sun on snow, Fagermo and Lindestad trudged up to No. 18. Fru Andersen and Fru Vibe were ensconced in the doorway, deep in the only topic Bergen people do talk about when they get together, a nostalgic ramble through their rainy home city. They gave it up for business, however, on the approach of the two men.

'Look at that,' said Fru Vibe to Lindestad, whose tolerant expression told of years of dealing with complaining tenants. 'And you said it had been properly cleaned.'

'It was cleaned after the last tenants left,' said Lindestad, edging his way into the *vindfang*. 'That was last summer. You must expect a bit of dust.'

'That,' said Fru Andersen triumphantly, 'is not dust.'

Nor was it. It was a smallish, obstinate brown stain, clinging to wall and wooden skirting-board, just above floor level, and the lighter colour of the wall around told of Fru Andersen's Trojan endeavours to scrub it out.

'Let me see,' said Fagermo, and squatted down on his haunches in the tiny space. He needed little time to make up his mind. 'This mustn't be touched any further,' he said, getting up.

'Not touched?' howled Fru Andersen, outraged. 'But you can't expect—'

'Police,' said Fagermo, showing his card. 'This *must* not be touched. I'll have a man out to look at it in an hour or so. He'll have to take some sort of sample. Luckily there's still enough there to make tests on.'

'Tests?' said Fru Vibe, agog with interest. 'Then it *is* blood?'

185

'I think so.'

'I wondered,' she said. 'That's why I rang. Do you think it's that boy?' She nodded her head in the direction of the mountains.

Fagermo looked at her with interest: a handsome, intelligent-looking woman. 'Perhaps. It's what I'm working on. Had you any reasons for thinking it might be?'

'Oh no. It's just that since he was found, so close to here, we've all had rather a creepy feeling. And then when there was this blood . . .'

'But this house was empty, wasn't it, in December?' Fru Vibe nodded. 'Did you hear anything from next door?'

'Not a thing,' said Fru Vibe. 'It was winter, Christmas. You sort of shut yourself away at that time of year.' And as the reality of the thing struck her, she shivered. 'I don't understand.'

'Nor do I,' said Fagermo. And as he turned to go towards the car, leaving Lindestad to cope with the protests of Fru Andersen at being moved into a blood-stained house which seemed likely to be infested by policemen, he stood in the street, looking down the road at the other blocks and muttered: 'I think I'm going to have to do some research into these houses.'

CHAPTER 16

ILLUMINATION

The University Library, two floors down from Department of Languages and Literature, where Professor Nicolaisen had his office, presented next morning a fairly somnolent appearance. There were no students around: perhaps they were at lectures, or perhaps they never came. A few hen-like women scuttled around from shelves to catalogue clutching cards, books and periodicals, and having a frail, burdened look, as if the world were too much for them. An enquiry to the two pregnant ladies on the desk resulted in Fagermo being shown into the back room where Elisabeth Leithe worked. One glance at her was enough to dispel any idea of her as a conceivable murderess. She was barely five foot four, thin and pathetic, wearing a dreary nondescript cardigan over a nondescript dress, and having a dreary, washed-out face over a nondescript body. Fagermo tried to imagine a murder in which she took an active role: imagined Martin Forsyth obligingly kneeling on the floor of the *vindfang* while she swung a blunt instrument and bashed the back of his skull. The idea was absurd. Even as he turned into the doorway she was sitting at her desk, seeming merely to peer over it, and contemplating several piles of books waiting to have something done to them. Her eyes were great wet globes, as if somehow too much was being expected of her by someone or other. Fagermo introduced himself, sat down, and weighed straight in.

'I understand you live in the flat downstairs in Isbjørnvei 18, is that right?'

The creature looked at him fearfully, her wet, bulbous eyes almost obsessively fixed on his face. She nodded.

'Were you there on December the twenty-first?'

The girl thought, and then shook her head with a little high grunt that Fagermo took to be a negative.

'Where were you?'

'I went home. I had back holidays due to me. I had permission.' The words came out in a terrified squeak. Fagermo had the idea that she thought the university had put him on to her for taking unauthorized holidays.

'I see. So the house has been unoccupied since—when? When did you leave?'

'The fourteenth. I had permission. I had—'

'Yes, yes. I understand. When did you come back?'

'January the fourth.'

'Was everything all right in the house? You didn't notice anything changed?'

The terrified, rabbity face shook in wonderment.

'Nothing in your flat, anyway. I suppose you didn't go into the main part of the house?'

The girl swallowed and hesitated. 'I did. Because . . . I'm alone, alone in the house, I have been for months. I get . . . frightened. I went through the house when I came back, to make sure . . .'

'That you were still alone. Very sensible. Quite understandable. And there wasn't anything odd that you noticed?'

The head shook again.

'There was a brown stain in the *vindfang* when I was there yesterday. Have you noticed it?' She nodded. 'When was it, precisely, that you first saw it?'

'I noticed it soon after I came back. In January.'

'You didn't think anything of it?'

'No. I thought Lindestad must have been showing somebody over the house. He does sometimes. Or I thought I must have spilt something there, but I couldn't think what.'

Fagermo looked at the great dim eyes and got up to go. There was nothing to be got out of her. As he thanked her and began to slip unobtrusively through the door, her squeaky voice shrilled out: 'What was it?'

'Eh?'

'What was it? The brown stain?'

'Blood,' said Fagermo, and was thus directly responsible for a long, hag-ridden night of hideous dreams filled with vampires and rapists and fiendish torturers—dreams which led to another phone call to the harassed Lindestad, with a hysterical demand for a change of flat.

But Lindestad's obligingness and omnicompetence were put to a further test before that. Fagermo rang him up when he got back to the office with the fruits of his meditations overnight.

'Those houses in Isbjørnvei,' he said. 'I suppose all the keys are different?'

'Well, of course.'

'But each of the houses will have had a fair number of tenants in its time?'

'Depends. Some of the people stay a long time, others are only short-term—either because they're not permanent in Tromsø or because they want to buy themselves a house here. So some of the houses have the same tenants they've had since they were built four or five years ago, but others have had a long line of them.'

'Including number eighteen, perhaps?'

'Yes—there've been a fair few there.'

'And what happens to their keys when they leave?'

'They deliver them back to us, of course.'

'Only sometimes they've lost one, perhaps?'

'Oh yes, it happens. People are careless. It doesn't matter much to us: we can get more made.'

'And so can they, of course: get further keys made while they are tenants, and keep one.'

'They could,' said Lindestad, sounding bewildered. 'It's not something we've ever thought of. There wouldn't be much point unless they intended to rob the people who came in afterwards. As far as I know, not many of our professors have burglary as a sideline, though I'd be willing to believe anything about some of them.'

'Not burglary, no. Still, it's an interesting thought. Now—could you give me a list of all the people who've lived in number eighteen since it was built?'

'I could try. We've got the records, of course, but I could probably do it in my head. Could you give me half an hour?'

'All the time in the world. Think about it and get it right. I'm just collecting information.'

And collecting information was what Fagermo did most of over the next few days. Dribs from here, drabs from there. Phone calls here, tentative letters of enquiry there, resulting in little piles of paper on his desk, notes in a grubby notebook he had kept in his trouser pocket throughout the case and had made scrawls in, decipherable only by himself. And in the end they really did begin to make a pattern: Lindestad's lists: the reports from Interpol; the lists of people employed by British Petroleum and other major oil firms; the information from the Continental Shelf Research Institute. And then there was that very interesting conversation on the telephone with the man in State Oil, the Norwegian national oil company. He had been very cagey, of course: had displayed all the caution of the natural bureaucrat, one of the worst species of *homo sapiens* a policeman has to deal with. Nothing must go down on paper, that had to be made clear. Everything he said was off the record—right? And so on, and so on. But in the end he had unbuttoned at least one little corner of his mouth, and Fagermo and he had had a very interesting conversation.

There were still many, many minor aspects of the case to be attended to. It was going to take time, lots of time. Fagermo was a Norwegian. He liked taking his time. Before the real grind of routine investigation set in, though, there was one more brick to be placed in position, one very important thing to be attended to.

Dr Dougal Mackenzie lived in a handsome white wooden house towards the top of the island. Spacious, attractive, often old farms, some of them built by profiteers from the First World War, these houses were prized by some for their style, despised by others for their draughts, their inconveniences, the expense of their upkeep. Like most of the old wooden houses in Tromsø, they were in daily risk of burning down, either through faulty wiring or at the hands of the Town Council's official pyromaniac. But they were stylish, satisfying places to live in for people with the means to maintain them. Fagermo noted as he walked up the drive a man odd-jobbing around the well-shrubbed garden who was not Dougal Mackenzie. The snow lay now, in this first week of May, only in odd, obstinate patches in shady corners. Spring was beginning its long, flirtatious love-affair with the people of Tromsø.

Fagermo's ring on the door-bell was the signal for excited little whines and yelps on the other side, and—when the door was opened—for a doggy onrush, indiscriminate shows of friendliness, jumpings up and attempts to lick his face. After this, Jingle departed down the path to inspect the course of Fagermo's footprints and do a routine check around the murkier parts of the garden—for all the world as if he were a police constable.

Dougal Mackenzie seemed used to taking second place to his dog at the moment of opening the door. He appeared to take Fagermo's visit equably, but his eyebrows were raised quizzically when he spoke.

'Well, Inspector, what can I do for you?' He held the door as if uncertain whether to invite him in or not.

'Could we have a chat for a little, do you think?'

'By all means.' Mackenzie—smiling and friendly, and quite unlike Sidsel Korvald in his reception of a police visit—opened the door wide and ushered him into the house, pausing only to call Jingle in from a distant lilac bush, and then make futile attempts to persuade him on to his chair.

The sitting-room was pleasantly furnished in a modern style of comfort which did not clash too obtrusively with the traditional air of the house. English newspapers littered the side tables, and dotted around other spaces in the room were files, open books, and what looked like drafts of examination papers. It was the house of a busy, untidy academic.

'Sorry about this,' said Dougal Mackenzie. 'Bit of a mess, I'm afraid. My wife is sick.'

'Oh dear—anything serious?'

'Not really. Finds it difficult to adapt, you know. Had to have a spell in hospital in February. I've packed her off to Scotland for a month or two. Should set her up.'

Fagermo had been in Scotland, and had his own opinions of what a couple of months in that country in springtime would do to a person, but he held his peace. He knew that some foreigners, and many Norwegians too, did find it difficult to adapt to the darkness of a Northern winter, particularly in their second or third year.

'That's sad,' he said. 'I hope she perks up.'

'Oh, these things—' said Mackenzie, flapping his hand vaguely towards an armchair unencumbered with papers or files. 'Luckily I'm used to looking after myself.'

'Oh yes—when you've been living abroad, I suppose.'

'That's right,' said Mackenzie. He said it with an American intonation: That's *right*. 'What was it you wanted to see me about? It's a long time now since I found the body. I don't suppose there's anything new I can add.'

'No, no—probably not. No, I'm really consulting you in your official capacity.'

'What do you mean? As an academic?'

'Exactly. You see, I'm a pretty unscientific person. A bit of a disadvantage these days for a policeman: mostly when we solve a crime it's the boffins who do the lion's share of the detection. So I trail along with the good old human factor. And when you said you were a marine geologist I didn't immediately connect you with oil.'

'Really?' said Mackenzie, an open smile spreading over his plump, pink face. 'Lots of other things as well, of course, but to be sure oil is among them— especially up here. I'm sorry. I didn't realize the name didn't mean anything to you, otherwise I'd have said something when we talked about oil in the Cardinal's Hat the other week. You know how it is: I just didn't want—'

'To teach your grandmother to suck eggs, isn't that the English expression? No, I quite see. My own fault entirely. But it might mean that you can help me a lot: fill me in on the background. I've had a lot of help from the Continental Shelf people down in Trondheim, as a matter of fact.'

'Oh, yes—some first-rate people down there. And of course he'd worked there—hadn't he?'

'Yes, he had, actually. But there are some other things I thought you were probably the best person to come to for. For example, he'd worked, as you say, on boats with the Continental Shelf research people. Collecting data, and so on—most of it done electronically, with pretty sophisticated equipment. How much do you think all that data they collected would have meant to a chap like that—a chap with a respectable but fairly ordinary education?'

'Little or nothing, as a general rule.'

'Even if he'd worked in oil before?'

'Oh yes, even then. You need a real grounding in the subject—from a university or polytechnic in fact—before the sort of info they're getting would mean a thing. It's the sort of education we're aiming to provide here. And of course, even then the data by itself is nothing: you'd need time to work on it, even if you were an expert. You'd have to sit on all the stuff for a while before you could really assess its significance.'

'So normally all the data they collected would go straight to, say, State Oil, and even then they'd often call in expert advice, from the universities or wherever.'

'That's about it. It's a long job.'

'The end result being a better idea of the most profitable areas for drilling?'

'Yes—put very simply, that is one of the things they're interested in.'

'And not just State Oil.'

'Well, no. You know the way of the world, Inspector. There's a pretty cut-throat competition among the oil companies, and the gentlemanly rules sometimes get passed by. Don't they always? And particularly now, with the Middle-East supply getting more and more uncertain, everyone's interested in the North Sea fields. Particularly the Northern ones.'

'Why particularly the Northern ones?'

'Because they're so rich. That's one of the things we're pretty sure about. Enormously rich—much more so than the fields further south, the ones between Norway and Britain. And then, they represent the future—they will probably be the next big ones to be opened up. But there are so many imponderables: the cost of getting at it is one big one; then the technical difficulties due to the rugged weather; the political opposition to it from people up here; the opposition of the ecology people. It's all very exciting, just because it is so uncertain. So naturally all the various companies are interested in just about every aspect of what's going on, and what's being found out.'

'I see. That's roughly what I thought. But now, where do the universities come in?'

'Well, not as directly as the Continental Shelf people. But the fact is, this discovery of the North Sea oil found Norway pretty unprepared in a lot of ways. It was like a big pools win, you know. It wasn't something anyone could predict, or that you could do anything about in advance. So suddenly there was this big need for experts—in all the related fields. What's happened has been enormous expansion in the relevant university departments, with lots of money from the government to push it along. In the early years Norway has had to rely on a lot of foreign advice— Americans, Britons, Dutch, and so on. But Norway's in the grip of the same sort of petty nationalism as everyone else is these days: foreign help isn't good for national pride: she wants to breed her own experts and run her own show.'

'But meanwhile?'

'Meanwhile she still often has to call in experts from abroad to train the Norwegian experts of the future.'

'Hence you?'

Dr Mackenzie smiled broadly and leaned back on the sofa, stroking the head of his dog, who had given up all idea of going on his own chair and had finally jumped on the sofa and settled down with a sigh of boredom by the side of his master. 'Hence me, as you say. There are lots like me in Norwegian universities—in geology departments and elsewhere.'

'People with foreign experience?'

'Yes—people with foreign degrees, people with lectureships at foreign universities who can get a step up by coming to Norway. We've got in while the going's good, of course. In a few years they'll very likely be restricting jobs to Norwegian applicants.'

'I see. And you teach, supervise—you also act as consultants for State Oil now and then, I suppose.'

'Yes, now and then.'

'So in many ways you're key people in this whole business of North Sea oil?'

'Oh, I wouldn't say that. The key men are all down in Oslo, within State Oil. They're the ones who make the decisions. They've multiplied like rabbits down there in recent years, and I must say—well, perhaps I'd better not. One learns to be tactful after a time.'

'You think they're inefficient?'

Dr Mackenzie smiled and held his peace.

'Still,' said Fagermo, 'if you're not the key figures,

here in the universities, still you have a lot of sensitive information going through your hands.'

'Yes, I suppose so, now and then.'

'Information that a lot of people outside the system would give a packet to get their hands on?'

'I think you're being a little melodramatic there, Inspector. There are various ways of getting this information. Companies can mount research operations of their own, for example.'

'Illegally, surely, if they were within the Norwegian sphere of interest?'

'Yes, surely. But it happens. You've just got to look at the Russian fishing fleet . . .'

'Yes—that's the local joke, of course. Still, the big oil companies at least would prefer not to do anything so flagrantly illegal as mount their own operations, if it could be avoided. If there were other ways of getting hold of the sort of information they're after—'

'Well, yes, I suppose they'd take it, if there was no great risk involved.'

'Yes,' said Fagermo. 'So I would have thought. And a large wad of money to one or two people is in any case cheaper than an elaborate and clandestine scientific expedition.'

'No doubt. Though as I say, I don't think you should dramatize this too much. The State Oil people do a lot of sharing of information, when it suits them, and most of the data from these geological surveys gets around eventually.'

'Eventually. That may be the crucial point. Where there's a lot of money to be made, the various parties will want all the information they can get, and they'll want it fast. Hence the Russian fishing-boats, I suppose. But really, what I'm trying to do now is what I've been doing all along: fill in on Martin Forsyth. The boy and his background. See what possibilities he had for getting into trouble. Because one of the few things we know about him is that he certainly did get into trouble. One possibility was—still is—sex. But the difficulty with that is: he was here for such a short time. Another possibility is money. But then the question arises: what from? As far as I'm concerned the two most likely answers are spying—political spying— and oil.'

Dougal Mackenzie looked thoughtful. 'There have been some pretty odd deaths in the area, haven't there? Those Japanese or Chinese or whatever down near Bodø: they were never identified. People talked about spying, I remember.'

'They certainly did. It's the sort of thing people say when they don't know anything definite but think there's something mysterious going on. But nobody ever identified those foreigners. With Martin Forsyth we had the advantage of identifying him pretty easily. And then we found—amid lots of uncertainties—some backgound in oil. Here in Norway, both in the Stavanger set-up, and in Trondheim. And also in the Middle East. I soon found out that he'd probably worked in Abadan.'

'Really?'

'Yes. And as far as I'm concerned that seems to mean one thing: if there was anyone working on that boat doing geological surveys who was likely to know what he was doing, it was Forsyth. He was intelligent, he had a moderately good educational background— and above all he was sharp: he had a keen eye for the main chance, and he seemed to want to use it to make money quick.'

'Yes, I see,' said Mackenzie. 'That does seem to add up to a fair conclusion.'

'Doesn't get me far enough, though,' said Fagermo. 'If Forsyth was feeding information direct to—say—an American oil company, why should they kill the goose that was laying the golden eggs, or why should anyone else? It seemed to me that the situation was a bit more complex than that.'

He sat back, took out a cigarette, and lit it. 'Now, Dr Mackenzie, these foreigners who come and work in oil in this country, or in the universities, what is their background as a rule?'

'Well, as I say, they come here mostly for promotion. Norway needs people in a variety of fields connected in one way or another with oil: geologists of various kinds, geographers, economists with rather special interests—and plenty of others. Where you get a sudden demand like that you'll always get people applying from outside who think they'll get ahead faster abroad than they will in their own countries. Nobody likes being stuck on the lower rungs of the academic ladder when the only chance of rising is by stepping into dead men's shoes.'

'You're implying that most of them come direct from foreign universities, aren't you? But that's not always true, is it? Some have come here whose main experience is with overseas oil companies, isn't that right?'

'Oh, yes, certainly.'

'As in your own case, Dr Mackenzie.'

Dougal Mackenzie sat back in his sofa, his hand

once more on his dog's head, his whole body lazily drooping over the arm in a way designed to suggest relaxation. He smiled faintly. 'Yes, that's quite right. I had a period with one of the big British oil companies and another short spell with an American one. Most of us have, as you say, been with them at one time or another.'

'So I gather,' said Fagermo. 'It must make you very useful when it comes to all this consultation work.'

Mackenzie shrugged. 'Perhaps. They come to me—the State Oil people—now and then. All of us in geology departments who have this sort of special knowledge are used from time to time. Most of us have done our stint with the big oil people.'

'Again, so I gather,' said Fagermo. 'You, I believe, were working in Abadan for about five years before you came here.'

'That's right. Something like five, I suppose. In a way I expect you could say it was that experience got me this job. Naturally if they start drilling up here, someone with first-hand experience on the spot will be worth his weight.'

'Very nice,' said Fagermo, keeping his eye on that carefully relaxed body. 'Well—you can understand my interest. Martin Forsyth's mother says he worked at "Aberfan" or some such place as that. You've worked at Abadan—'

Dougal Mackenzie laughed and spread out his hands. 'Have you any *idea*, Inspector, of the size of the place, of how many foreigners work in or around Abadan?'

'A good many, I've no doubt. I presume you would deny that you ever met Martin Forsyth there?'

'Certainly I would—there or anywhere else as far as I remember. But one met a great number of people out there—many of them British. And remember that I only saw him dead here. But as far as I know, certainly I never met him. You've got to remember these oil companies are pretty stratified little societies. I don't want to sound snobbish, but Marty Forsyth and I would have moved in very different circles.'

'I notice you call him Marty. And yet I've never used that form in talking about him with you.'

'Martin—Marty. It's a common abbreviation.'

'Is it, sir? I'd like to check up on that. I had an idea that it was fairly unusual—more of a pet name, or a joke name based on a television star than a common abbreviation. Well, well—interesting. Now, one more little thing. Our medics are agreed that Forsyth was not killed where he was found—he was taken there later, after the blood on the wound had already congealed. Now, by pure luck—and it's about the only piece of luck we've had in this case—Forsyth had an unusual blood-group: he was AB positive. And the other day we were put on to a nasty bloodstain in the *vindfang* of Isbjørnvei 18. It was the same blood-group. And when I looked up the names of the people who had been tenants of number 18, I found your name, sir.'

'My dear Inspector, you're on to a loser there. That was all of three years ago. The first couple of months I spent here, before I bought this house.'

'Exactly, sir. I know the dates. But the idea I'm playing with is this: if you *should* have planned to kill this boy, you would hardly have wanted to use your own house, would you? Quite apart from the obvious danger of his being traced here, your wife was with you at the time, wasn't she? And yet you would want an address to give him, somewhere to meet him: he would have been highly suspicious of an outdoor tryst at that time of year. Now if it *should* happen that you had still got a key to the house in Isbjørnvei—one you thought you'd lost, and which therefore hadn't been returned to the University Administration—what better place to appoint to meet him than a house you knew was empty, and which you could get into. Around Christmas there's very few in those houses: a lot of tenants have gone to their families in other parts of Norway. It's dark by two, and most people huddle inside. Really, a very good place to kill.'

Dougal Mackenzie's smile had not relaxed, and if there seemed a new tenseness in the body he nevertheless gave an impression of relief that things had come into the open, a readiness to accept a challenge and enjoy a duel.

'Well, well, at last you've said it out,' he said. 'Fantastic as it all is, I know now exactly what you're thinking and suggesting. Let's take it from there: I know what I'm being accused of, and you know that I know. I think there's a distinct lack of anything in the way of evidence in your case so far, and the whys and wherefores are still a mystery.'

'You're right,' agreed Fagermo amiably. 'Quite right. Very little evidence. Only very tenuous indications. Little connections like spiders' webs. Now, here's another little dribble of information. As you say, the people at State Oil often use the high-ups at the universities as consultants to evaluate the data collected on these various research expeditions in the

North Sea. But well over a year ago, they stopped using you.'

'But, Inspector, this isn't a regular thing. There are
several of us. This sort of work goes in fits and starts.'

'Quite possibly. But they *deliberately* stopped using
you. There are several Professors and Readers in your
field previously employed by one or other of the big
oil companies. For various reasons—mainly, of course,
the suspicion that some companies were acting on information which they shouldn't have had—they began
to have doubts about the reliability of some of the
people they were using. Because this stuff was definitely confidential. So they began making little tests.
And as a result, a couple of people were dropped as
consultants. One of them was you.'

'I see. Well, this is news to me. It seems rather like
condemnation without trial. And, with all due respect,
I still don't entirely see the significance.'

'End of useful extra income,' said Fagermo, with his
most urbane smile. 'And I don't mean the payment
from State Oil for your consultancy work: eighty per
cent of that would go back in income tax at your sal-
ary level. But why else would you have been passing
on information except for money? What was threatened was that extra whack you have been getting, tax
free, from whichever company, or compan*ies*, you
were passing on the information to. I don't know the
rate for the game, but I'd have thought these must
have been tidy sums, to make it worth your while.'

'You have, I suppose, Inspector, some shreds of *evidence* that this is what I've been doing?'

'Quite frankly, no, sir,' said Fagermo, with undimin-
ished amiability. 'As you will be aware, this is an area

where we can't get information by our normal channels. Nothing short of a Congressional Committee or a Royal Commission or something of that sort could get details of the sort of payment I'm thinking of: undercover payment by one of the big multi-nationals. So you're quite right: here we are definitely moving into the realms of conjecture.'

'Have we ever been out of it? Still, go on and entertain me further.'

'Well, I'm quite willing to acknowledge that what I'm suggesting here is sheer guesswork. We'll keep it on that level. I think that somewhere around this time, when you stopped being used by the State Oil people, you met up again with Martin Forsyth—if in fact you'd ever lost touch. For all I know you could have got him his first job in this country with the oil people down in Stavanger, but that's not a vital part of the story. I think it occurred to you, when you met up with him, that there were other ways of getting the gen the oil companies wanted than by having it referred to you as consultant. If you had somebody bright, sharp, somebody with experience and a bit of grounding in the subject, and if he got a job with one or other of the bodies doing the geological surveying, then you could go on with your little side-line. Splitting the proceeds, of course, with your partner, doubtless in some such proportion as eighty per cent to you and twenty to him. That was your downfall.'

'You've given me precious little reason to think I've fallen down so far.'

'In the first instance *his* downfall, of course. But eventually yours. I'll see to that. For some while I'd guess the scheme worked very well: Forsyth got the job with the Continental Shelf Research people. They were very happy to have him: he was significantly better than the men they usually recruited as hands on their boats. Suspicious in itself, I think. I've found out they were paying him decidedly *less* than he was getting in Stavanger, and my impressions of the sort of chap Forsyth was suggest that he wasn't one to take a pay cut just for the joy of working on boats. Everyone says he was a loner, a reserved sort of boy, but one who knew what he was doing. I feel pretty sure that what he was doing was feeding all the information he could get hold of to you. And that you were doing what he wasn't qualified to do: interpreting it, and feeding it forward to one or other—perhaps more than one—of the big oil companies. Conceivably even to the Russians as well, who have oil interests of their own in the Barents Sea, and are very interested in everything Norway is doing in the way of oil exploration.'

'Quite a lucrative little side-line. You make it sound as if the whole of the world's oil industry was knocking at my door and stuffing money through my letter-box.'

'Not quite—but I should think you did very well. The big companies have a pretty good network of contacts, covering any area where they have an interest, or hope to have an interest: local politicos (I think they have one here); academics; journalists; any sort of leader of local opinion. They're interested in information, and they're also interested in shaping local feeling towards the coming of oil, and towards their own claims. I think they pay well.'

'But from your point of view it's frustrating that it's so difficult to get proof, I should think?'

'Very frustrating. But I'll go on with those little cobwebs of suggestions. When we look at you and your life-style, we can't help but wonder, sir. It's not many academics can afford these old wooden houses, particularly one as large and handsome as this. It's one of the best specimens in Tromsø. Then, you've got a large Swedish car, and more recently you've acquired a boat. Somehow all this takes you just that bit out of the academic rut as far as life-style is concerned—it's more the very prosperous doctors and lawyers, or the really successful businessmen who run to houses like this, to boats the size of yours.'

'Of course, you know nothing about my personal background, about my family, and so on.'

'I will, sir, I will. Did you inherit money? Did you make a lot when you were with oil, and did you save it? I'll be looking at all that. I'll be looking at your bank accounts—not your Norwegian ones: those are too easy, too open to inspection. But somehow or other I'll have to get a look at your British ones, possibly an American one, a continental one? It won't be easy. Perhaps it will be impossible. But I've set things in motion already, and I think in the long term I'll get results.'

There was a silence as Dougal Mackenzie contemplated, still with a slight, thin smile on his lips, the long term opening up before him. His dog, Jingle, was now resting his head on his lap, seeming pleased with the restfulness of the conversation.

'You haven't explained,' said Dr Mackenzie at last,

'why I should kill this boy. Does your little trip into fantasy not include motivation? I should have thought it was the last thing I'd want to do if I was using him to make money out of all and sundry.'

'I think that's quite easy, if you take in the human factor. I think you were two of a mind. Like you, Martin Forsyth could never get enough. You used him. I expect you despised him. You thought that because he had no academic background he was stupid, that he would be an easy tool. But Martin Forsyth was nobody's tool. And he wasn't stupid, though he was very, very unwise. You both slipped up on the human factor: if you had underestimated him, he certainly underestimated you. I think quite early on in the game he realized that he *was* being used; that provided he could make contacts higher up he could feed the information *direct* to the various potential customers, without having you as middleman, since it could be interpreted at base there. But above all he realized that now you'd entered into this arrangement with him, you'd put yourself in his power. It's something middle-class people almost always forget.'

'What is?'

'That if you *use* someone like Martin Forsyth, you're using someone who has nothing to lose—no stable job, no "respectability", no reputation. Whereas someone like you, sir, has all of those things, and doesn't want to lose them. It puts you in his power.'

'I should have thought an academic these days was one of the most generally despised members of the community,' said Dougal Mackenzie, his smile broader than ever.

'Ah—that's just your little academic joke. In fact, an

academic has an almost impregnable position. Perhaps that's what attracted you, after serving with the oil companies. You're virtually impossible to sack, however incompetent. You're actually looked up to by a lot of people, at least here in Norway: it's very much a "status" job, and in a country with no aristocracy, it's the people in the status jobs who are the cream of the cream. It's something you people in the university come to take for granted. I've heard a left-wing academic complain bitterly that when he went to jail for drunken driving he was put in with common criminals. He thought he could shelter behind some impregnable bourgeois fortress. No, the fact is that you had everything to lose, and Forsyth had nothing.'

'You're saying, if I understand you right, that he blackmailed me. No doubt you hope my bank account will bear this out too.'

'Possibly it will. More probably not. Because I should think this was just the beginning. He can't have been feeding you information for many months, and he'd need a really good hold over you. And, as for you, you'd realize as soon as the first hint of blackmail was made that this was something that could go on for ever. I think the sequence was this: Forsyth began with oblique approaches, you spotted his game from the beginning, and made an appointment in Isbjørn-vei to talk things over.'

'And there killed him?'

'Yes. I think he came up here a day or two early, to spy out the land and think things over. I don't know what he'd decided on when he went to the appointment, but I guess he was hardly in the door before you killed him, quickly and quietly.'

'I see—the blood in the *vindfang*. You're building an awful lot on very little, Inspector.'

'I know, I know,' said Fagermo. 'I'm telling you my thoughts, not making out a case. I'm just at the beginning. There's going to be months of rummaging around after proofs. Now—as I say, I take it you hit him hard as he was turning to take his coat off in the hall, and that he fell backwards into the *vindfang*—hence the bloody mark. Then I think you pulled him into the hall or one of the downstairs rooms and stripped his clothes off.'

'To hinder identification, I suppose?'

'Of course. That was very important. There's one interesting thing there. You stripped off not just his clothes, but also his ring. That must have been difficult to get off: it was tight, and left a deep ridge. A nasty, sick-making process, I think, for someone who wasn't a natural murderer. I've been mentioning rings to a lot of people, on the assumption that a once-off murderer would remember that most of all. I sensed a reaction when I mentioned it in the Cardinal's Hat, and I fancy it was *you* who reacted. You hadn't banked on the ring.'

'Hadn't banked on it?'

'I mean that not many ordinary young men in Britain wear rings. You hadn't expected it. But he was engaged—sort of—to a Norwegian girl, and she did what any Norwegian girl would do: she bought him a ring. And so you had to tug and tug to get it off. And you remembered that in the Cardinal's Hat. I think you are remembering it now.'

A flicker of emotion had passed over Dougal Mackenzie's face. He said quickly, 'And so I went and buried him in the snow, only to decide to discover him there three months later.'

'Well, oddly enough, as it turned out—yes.'

'I've heard of murderers revisiting the scene of the crime, but other than Burke and Hare I've not heard of them burying the body and then enthusiastically digging it up again. It sounds more like my dog than me.'

Jingle looked up at the mention of his kind, and tentatively wagged his tail.

'Told like that it sounds absurd,' said Fagermo confidently. 'But what you're describing is what *happened*, not what you *wanted* to happen. Things didn't pan out as you expected on that occasion. As I say, I think the murder was a hurriedly planned affair. A quick response to a dangerous threat. You stripped the body of all identifying marks, and then—at night, probably—you took it a little way up in the mountains away from the houses and there buried it. It was snowing in any case. It must have been an easy job. But later I imagine you regretted it. Especially when that paragraph appeared in the papers about the boy missing from the Alfheim Pensjonat.'

'I don't actually read Norwegian, Inspector.'

'It was a topic of common gossip, especially among the British community. And when that came up, you realized there was a real danger if the body was discovered of its being identified; and if that happened, all sorts of connections might be made. Whereas if the body had been well weighted and thrown in the fjord, the chances are it would never have been found—or if it had been, it would have been totally unidentifiable. Difficult to do without detection from dry land; difficult to do from either of the bridges, because people keep a look-out for suicides, and anything suspicious might have been noticed. But I think that about this time the question began to nag you: was it too late? And in fact it was about this time, the end of February, that you bought the boat, wasn't it?'

'How well informed you are—already, Inspector.'

'I've checked what I *can* check here, sir. That was one of the things. Anyway, you bought the boat, and then one day early in March, shortly after the first thaw, you went to look at the state of the snow. I don't think you realized how much difference even a brief thaw makes to the snow levels. You went to satisfy yourself that you could get the body up with comparative ease—it was a reconnaissance trip. But in fact he was already practically exposed.'

'I could very easily have covered him over again, though.'

'But in fact you had the most awful luck, didn't you? I've read over the accounts again, and it's clear how it happened. Your dog started tugging at the ear in the snow, and just at that moment Captain Horten skied down the mountain and came to the spot. And the aggravating fellow stopped to look. From then on, your plan was sunk. Horten realized there was a body there, and all you could do was participate in the discovery. A good, innocent-seeming role for a murderer, but much, much less safe than the one you had planned. We have an awful lot to thank your dog for.'

Dougal Mackenzie's fondling of that dog's head was by now becoming somewhat obsessive, but he slept on, head in lap, oblivious of all except the sounds of interest to dogs—birds, barks, nature outside the window. He looked, in fact, rather pleased with himself. But then, the expression on Dougal Mackenzie's face was hardly less complacent.

'Well, sir,' said Fagermo, 'that basically is my case.'

'Your *case*, Inspector?'

'You're quite right. As I said before, it's not a case at all. Just a fantasy based on a few significant connections—Abadan, geological research for oil, number eighteen Isbjørnvei, the blood in the *vindfang* . . . just a series of slight, suggestive indications.'

'Wouldn't it have been better to wait until you'd got something more substantial? At the moment what you have is hardly, I would have thought, worth mentioning.'

'Right again, sir. Normally I would have got a great deal further before I even broached the subject. But then, normally any investigating I had to do would be within Norway—plodding work, painstaking details, but easy, open, accessible stuff. Now the investigation of this case is going to be very different. Heaven knows when—if ever—it's going to be possible to do any serious work in Iran. If it proves not to be, I'm going to make contacts with other people who were working for the same company—people on your own level, the sort of people who are getting out fast now. And perhaps I shall be able to find some who were friends of Forsyth, if he had any: he kept his cards close to his chest, that boy. Then of course there are the oil firms themselves, their central offices. And of course the consultancy work you did for State Oil here, and the reasons for their thinking you had been guilty of leaking information. Then, as I said, there are your own personal records—bank accounts, and so on.'

'What a long, tedious prospect seems to stretch in front of you, Inspector.'

'Very long. Not tedious, I hope. I expect at the end I shall be a lot better informed about the ways of the big world.'

'Very foolish of you to put me wise to what you are going to be doing before you even start, isn't it? There's no knowing what I mightn't be able to have destroyed.'

'Very unorthodox, certainly. But I had a reason. You see, I don't at this moment know the extent of your activities. I will, but I don't yet. This may be an iso-lated—lapse, shall we call it? Or you may have a much bigger thing going than I know about. More Martin Forsyths doing dirty work for you—picking up pocket money while you go off with the big sums. As long as you thought you were entirely in the clear in this case, that kind of thing could still be going on. And that meant this thing could happen over again.'

'You think I'm some kind of mass murderer or some-thing?'

'Anyone who has killed *can* kill again. And in fact, *they* might be in danger, *you* might be in danger. Things might work out very differently a second time. I don't give a hang about the grubby little spyings of the oil companies, or the Russians, or any other nation on earth. But I care about murder. Martin Forsyth may have been a contemptible little tick, but he had a right to go on breathing beyond his twenty-third year.'

Fagermo got up, smiled at his antagonist, and began to move towards the door.

'So what I've been saying has been in the nature of a warning. You're being watched. All the time I'm engaged in this long, detailed investigation, you'll be watched. You can't take one step outside the strict path of the law without it being known. As long as you realize this, everyone will be a lot safer. I know there's no sort of court case to be made out of a few slips of the tongue on your part: Marty for Martin; knowing he'd worked for the Continental Shelf people in Trondheim when you shouldn't. Easy as pie to make up a story to cover that sort of lapse. But I'll be going round the world, looking at records, talking to people who knew you during your days in big business. I'll be talking to your colleagues here, your bank managers. I'll be uncovering every little thing about you, down to the last detail. I'm afraid I'll have to talk to your wife too. She was in fact in Aasgård, wasn't she, sir, the mental hospital? Did she have her suspicions of you, perhaps? I'll be gentle with her, but I'm afraid I'll have to talk to her. Because there *is* a case to be made. And I assure you, I'm going to make it.'

They arrived at the front door, and Dougal Mackenzie held it open with theatrical politeness and stood framed in it while Fagermo made his way down the front steps, Jingle at his feet still looking friendly and wagging his tail in ignorant good will.

'I suppose the only thing to do is wish you a pleasant time in your researches, Inspector,' Mackenzie said, raising his voice above the traffic noises from the street below. 'A pleasant time, not a successful one.' He paused and went on: 'Of course, if this were

215

a book, what I'd say at this point would be "All right, Fagermo, you win", or something fatuous like that. They always give in so easily in books, don't they?'

'Often in life too, Dr Mackenzie,' said Fagermo. 'You'd be surprised.'

'Well, I'm not going to oblige with any such cliché. So I'll just wish you a thoroughly gruelling and frustrating next few weeks, Inspector.'

Fagermo grinned amiably at him, and ambled off towards the front gate. But when he got there, he turned.

'Of course, you're quite right,' he said. 'It is a cliché from books, nothing more. But you know, it really would be better if you did just what you say. Much better—for you, your wife, for everyone. It sounds silly, but you'd be much happier in the long run.'

He paused a moment, but his eyes met with no change in Dougal Mackenzie's arrogant smile. With a sigh he turned on his heel and made for his car.

CHAPTER 17

MIDNIGHT SUN

Early one evening, when term was over and June well advanced, Dougal Mackenzie—having pecked uninterestedly at his evening meal, and cast an eye over the newspaper headlines—put Jingle on a lead, gathered his various bowls and sources of entertainment into a plastic bag, and took him round to his neighbour's.

'It *is* all right, isn't it?' he asked.

'Of *course*,' said his neighbour, a comfortable, fat Norwegian lady in the prime of widowhood. 'For as long as you like. Take a really good break. You've been looking tired lately, I said so to my daughter. It's a long term, isn't it, spring term? Take a good holiday. He's always welcome here.'

And Jingle, having extracted the maximum of dramatic pathos out of saying farewell at the gate, went wagtailing it around the garden, determined to establish for himself from the beginning a regime of the utmost permissiveness.

Dougal Mackenzie went back home, got one or two necessaries, then got into his gleaming Volvo stationwagon and drove towards town. It sped along, with no more noise or friction than if it had been an arrow speeding towards some half-seen target. Dougal

Mackenzie almost relaxed. A good car always made him feel good, and if it was his own good car he felt doubly good. It wasn't often recently that he had felt so nearly free.

He sped over the bridge, past the Arctic Cathedral, and finally left his car at the end of Anton Jakobsens-vei.

Superstitious, he said to himself.

There were plenty of points from which to begin a climb up the mountains, but somehow it had to be here. He had never thought of anywhere else but here.

As he took off from the road, up the path edged with stunted bushes and sturdy little trees, he neared the spot where the body of Martin Forsyth had been buried. He turned his head away. He had never offered so much as a mock-reproach to his dog about that finding of the body—a dog was a dog was a dog—but it was natural that as he went by the place his mind should play on what might have been, on what chance had done to him, on what might have happened.

But perhaps, he thought, it would all have come out the same in the end.

When he had managed the first stiff ascent he stopped and looked down. Parked not too far from his own car was another—anonymous, unobtrusive, but well-known to him. One man was still in the driver's seat. Another was standing by the passenger's door, smoking a cigarette and idly looking up. Dougal Mackenzie could just make out his thick, black, drooping moustache. He smiled, and turned his face upwards again.

It was odd how serene he felt, in the evening air, with the sun, bright and warm, streaming down on him. Odd how untroubled, unresentful, unregretful. His mind had somehow cleaned itself out. There were no 'if only's now; no curses against the greed of the boy; no sad backward glances at things he himself had botched. What was done was done. By now he no longer even felt he had any control over himself. He merely walked blindly ahead to an obscure destination—unclear, but safe. He patted his pocket.

Really, it wasn't the end that was unclear, but the beginning. When, where, had it all begun? Not at school, surely. He remembered himself as a thin, sickly schoolboy, inclined to priggishness and goody-goody friends. Surely that boy was not father to this man? He never remembered any fast bits of schoolboy commerce, any sharp cutting of corners. He wouldn't have dared.

University had liberated him from the priggishness, but he didn't remember dreaming of luxury, of the quick buck dubiously acquired. Perhaps it was the grinding three years afterwards, at Hull, as a research student. Prolonged penny-pinching maketh the heart sick.

But whenever it was, by the time he had come to work at Abadan it was there—gnawing, writhing inside him. A little worm of envy, of twisted ambition. Because as soon as he had met Martin Forsyth he had recognized him as a fellow, spotted the same disease in him. They had stood there one day, in the overwhelming morning heat in the dusty centre of the oil processing works—the thin, tough boy with the hard eyes and the workman's hands, and the pot-bellied executive, haltingly acquiring the manners of his middle-rank—and like had spoken to like, greed to greed. Dougal Mackenzie had not liked Martin Forsyth. He had recognized him.

After that they had never spoken often. They weren't, in the company structure, in the same class by a long chalk, and habit and convention set all sorts of barriers and gulfs between the minutely distinguishable grades. Nevertheless, he had once invited him home for a drink. He remembered him sitting there, making small-talk with off-hand confidence to him and his wife, yet all the time his eyes darting round the various objects in the room that bespoke Mackenzie's status, almost costing the furniture. His wife had said when he left that she thought him unlikeable, and he had agreed. It was true. He had not liked him. He had recognized him.

He paused half-way up the mountain. The bush and undergrowth around the path had given way momentarily to more open country, sloping green down to open fields, and presenting a vista of great glory. Below him, island, town, mainland and fjord came together to form a jigsaw more intricate and beautiful than human mind could devise, chamber music in green and white and gold. A valedictory spread.

In the very far distance he could see his own car, and the car that had been parked nearby. Now there was nobody standing beside it. Was he now inside? or had he begun to climb? Dougal Mackenzie smiled faintly, and patted his jacket pocket.

Funny, that was the last thing he remembered Forsyth doing. He was just about to take his anorak off, and patted his pocket as he did so. The papers were there—the last lot of data from the survey boat, the bone that was to be dangled before his eyes, the sweetener of the coming blackmail. He had got the papers easily enough, after he had hit him. After he had dragged him back into the hall. And before he had begun the grisly job of stripping the body—the job that had ended with his pulling, dragging like a maniac at his ring. Even now the sweat on his forehead was not from the heat of the sun.

That had been the last day of his peace. Before that the worm born in the black liquid wealth of Abadan had given him many good days. He had enjoyed his first months in Tromsø, settling into a stable, safe job, and the moderate luxury of a beautiful house, money to buy good Scandinavian furniture, a quiet, powerful car, the knowledge that his means could encompass most of what he could want, with ease. He had thought it a kindly worm. His wife, he thought, had been happy too those months.

But 'things' had turned against him. The safeness, the stability had been threatened before the first year was out. The worm had seemed less kindly, and had gone on gnawing. When the major threat came out into the open he had acted fast to preserve his safety, but he had preserved nothing. Even in those first weeks after the murder, nothing had been quite the same. His wife had suspected—suspected *something*. She had looked at him in a new way. She had known what Martin Forsyth was. Now she knew what he, her husband, had become.

One last half-hour's climb through steep terrain overgrown with bushes and growths which covered the path and he emerged at last on the uplands. He sat down for a minute on a ledge and got his breath back, but—restless—he got up almost at once and began walking again. The plateau stretched in rolling greens and browns, with the night sun streaming upon it and dancing in the occasional patch of water. He was in the open. He was free.

It was freedom, in fact, that he had lost. It was not only his conscience that the worm had eaten away, it was his freedom. Ringing him round over these last years with new fears, new unspeakable secrets, new hindrances to action. That was why, unconsciously, he had known it had to be up here—on the top of a glorious world, free of shackles and guilts. Just to have the illusion again for a few hours.

Because Fagermo had been wrong. It would not have been better to give up then, throw down the cards, admit it all. It would have been infinitely worse. Of course these last few weeks had been terrible, feeling the net tighten, every facet of his life under scrutiny. Yesterday had been the last straw, when he knew the inspector had been talking for hours about him with his own colleagues.

But there was a way of cutting the net. He knew that once his safe, respectable existence had been shattered there was no putting it together again. He had sometimes contemplated the careers of exposed civil servants, local councillors, Members of Parliament, whose financial malpractices had been revealed and prosecuted. What could they be when they emerged from jail but shifty, pathetic shells of people? Fagermo's way was no way. It led only to that. And there was something better open to him.

And as he wandered over the winding paths, around mounds and crags with occasional views, tantalizing, of distant islands looming over the fjord, he experienced again that subtle sense of freedom, that illusion of infinite possibilities.

Until suddenly, in the glare of midnight, he realized he was not alone. There in the distance, now visible, now hidden by the terrain, was a dark, bulky figure, watching him, following. His hours of freedom were over.

There was no regret. Mackenzie reached in his pocket, fondled the gun for a brief moment, then—hidden for a moment from his observer—carefully took it out. Experimentally he opened his mouth. The shot, when it came, was not loud—sounded indeed irrelevant in this natural vastness, a petty thing measured against the blaring trumpets of the sun.